"Marry Me, Lyn."

Lyn tugged her hand  around her body in a cursed himself for bei marry someone becaus with them."

He kept his voice low, soothing. "It's not that." He placed his hands on her upper arms. "Don't give me an answer now. Let me explain what I've been thinking."

"You don't have to feel responsible for me, Cal. I can take care of myself now."

"Lyn, I'd like very much for you to be my wife. I'd like to make a life for you, work this ranch and have children with you." He grinned. "You may even be pregnant now."

She blushed. "It's—it's a big step for me."

He understood. Marriage hadn't been a picnic for her the last time. "I'm not like your ex-husband, baby. I respect your opinions and I'd never mistreat you. I would...protect you."

Dear Reader,

Thanks to all who have shared, in letters and at our Web site, eHarlequin.com, how much you love Silhouette Desire! One Web visitor told us, "When I was nineteen, this man broke my heart. So I picked up a Silhouette Desire and…lost myself in other people's happiness, sorrow, desire.… Guys came and went and the books kept entertaining me." It is so gratifying to know how our books have touched and even changed your lives—especially with Silhouette celebrating our 20ᵗʰ anniversary in 2000.

The incomparable Joan Hohl dreamed up October's MAN OF THE MONTH. *The Dakota Man* is used to getting his way until he meets his match in a feisty jilted bride. And Anne Marie Winston offers you a *Rancher's Proposition,* which is part of the highly sensual Desire promotion BODY & SOUL.

First Comes Love is another sexy love story by Elizabeth Bevarly. A virgin finds an unexpected champion when she is rumored to be pregnant. The latest installment of the sensational Desire miniseries FORTUNE'S CHILDREN: THE GROOMS is *Fortune's Secret Child* by Shawna Delacorte. Maureen Child's popular BACHELOR BATTALION continues with *Marooned with a Marine.* And Joan Elliott Pickart returns to Desire with *Baby: MacAllister-Made,* part of her wonderful miniseries THE BABY BET.

So take your own emotional journey through our six new powerful, passionate, provocative love stories from Silhouette Desire—and keep sending us those letters and e-mails, sharing your enthusiasm for our books!

Enjoy!

Joan Marlow Golan

Joan Marlow Golan
Senior Editor, Silhouette Desire

Please address questions and book requests to:
Silhouette Reader Service
U.S.: 3010 Walden Ave., P.O. Box 1325, Buffalo, NY 14269
Canadian: P.O. Box 609, Fort Erie, Ont. L2A 5X3

Rancher's Proposition
ANNE MARIE WINSTON

Published by Silhouette Books
America's Publisher of Contemporary Romance

For Richard and Kathy Jobgen,
my "Kadoka Konnection,"
with gratitude and thanks for their patience and graciousness
in answering my endless idiotic city-girl questions.
For the many miles we traveled together and all the
people they shared with me.
Here's to friends, wherever they may be found.

 SILHOUETTE BOOKS

ISBN 0-373-76322-0

RANCHER'S PROPOSITION

Visit Silhouette at www.eHarlequin.com

Printed in U.S.A.

Books by Anne Marie Winston

Silhouette Desire

Best Kept Secrets #742
Island Baby #770
Chance at a Lifetime #809
Unlikely Eden #827
Carolina on My Mind #845
Substitute Wife #863
Find Her, Keep Her #887
Rancher's Wife #936
Rancher's Baby #1031
Seducing the Proper Miss Miller #1155
*The Baby Consultant #1191
*Dedicated to Deirdre #1197
*The Bride Means Business #1204
Lovers' Reunion #1226
The Pregnant Princess #1268
Seduction, Cowboy Style #1287
Rancher's Proposition #1322

*Butler County Brides

ANNE MARIE WINSTON

has believed in happy endings all her life. Having the opportunity to share them with her readers gives her great joy. Anne Marie enjoys figure skating and working in the gardens of her south-central Pennsylvania home.

IT'S OUR 20th ANNIVERSARY!
We'll be celebrating all year,
Continuing with these fabulous titles,
On sale in October 2000.

Desire

#1321 The Dakota Man
Joan Hohl

#1322 Rancher's Proposition
Anne Marie Winston

#1323 First Comes Love
Elizabeth Bevarly

#1324 Fortune's Secret Child
Shawna Delacorte

#1325 Marooned With a Marine
Maureen Child

#1326 Baby: MacAllister-Made
Joan Elliott Pickart

Romance

#1474 The Acquired Bride
Teresa Southwick

#1475 Jessie's Expecting
Kasey Michaels

#1476 Snowbound Sweetheart
Judy Christenberry

#1477 The Nanny Proposal
Donna Clayton

#1478 Raising Baby Jane
Lilian Darcy

#1479 One Fiancée To Go, Please
Jackie Braun

Special Edition

#1351 Bachelor's Baby Promise
Barbara McMahon

#1352 Marrying a Delacourt
Sherryl Woods

#1353 Millionaire Takes a Bride
Pamela Toth

#1354 A Bundle of Miracles
Amy Frazier

#1355 Hidden in a Heartbeat
Patricia McLinn

#1356 Stranger in a Small Town
Ann Roth

Intimate Moments

#1033 Who Do You Love?
Maggie Shayne/
Marilyn Pappano

#1034 Her Secret Weapon
Beverly Barton

#1035 A Thanksgiving to Remember
Margaret Watson

#1036 The Return of Luke McGuire
Justine Davis

#1037 The Lawman Meets His Bride
Meagan McKinney

#1038 The Virgin Beauty
Claire King

Prologue

He couldn't believe his sister had done this to him.

Cal McCall gritted his teeth and fumed silently as he regarded the woman standing before him. She was on the tall side for a woman, but even the oversize shirt and too-large jeans she wore couldn't disguise the stick-thin look of her. Her head was down, and a thick curly mane of dark red hair hid most of her face and half her upper body as she stood passive, unmoving, waiting for...for what?

Questions, he assumed. Instructions. He'd asked his sister to hire a housekeeper for him, so this was his own damned fault. Silver had the softest heart in South Dakota. She'd told him that Lyn Hamill needed a job and a place to stay when she was released from protective services; he, as far as his sister was concerned, was the perfect answer.

Again, his gaze ran over his new employee. Hell, she

didn't look well enough to be out of the hospital much less capable of taking care of the big old ranch house he'd recently purchased. He knew she'd been a victim of domestic abuse and he surely was sympathetic to her troubles, but he needed someone who could paint and wallpaper, someone who could scrub bathtubs and haul loads of laundry, keep a vegetable garden, herd cantankerous bulls and groom horses if need be. This woman looked like she'd need help even to groom herself.

"So," he heard himself say. "I, ah, I understand you want to work for me."

The head nodded, a slight movement that set the red curtain of her hair rippling, and copper sparks shot from it where the sun touched it. He had to restrain the urge to reach out and hook a finger through one of the curls that hung freely to well below her shoulders. One thing he'd say for her, she had pretty hair.

He sighed heavily. Silver had him between a rock and a hard place and she knew it. One of his dreams had been to buy back the ranch his daddy had owned. When the opportunity had arisen, he'd lunged at it, and Silver had pitched in to help him clean and redecorate the outdated old house. Unfortunately, she'd fallen for a neighboring rancher and gotten married before the job was done.

Still, he owed her for her help. And the only wedding gift she wanted from him was his promise to give this gal a chance.

"Well, I guess we can give it a shot," he said. "I'm finishing some remodeling, so there's going to be some mess and upheaval from time to time. And I'll need your help with a few outside chores as well." He paused, expecting a response, but she remained perfectly still. After the silence got awkward, he said, "Where are your things? I'll go ahead and load them while you say your goodbyes.''

The woman nodded again. Without raising her head, she pointed to a large paper bag with two handles and a familiar department store logo. It leaned drunkenly against one of the porch posts of the women's shelter where he'd come to pick up his new employee.

He looked at the bag, then at her. "This is it?" He'd never met a woman who could travel with less than six pair of shoes, ten pounds of cosmetics and major quantities of female junk. This single bag couldn't possibly be the only thing she was bringing.

''Are you ready to leave, dear?'' A big, plump woman wearing a pair of jeans that would fit a much smaller person clumped across the porch of the shelter for women in crisis situations. She wore an eye-popping electric pink blouse with a hefty belt of beaten silver cinched tightly around her, and when she folded his silent companion against her ample bosom, Lyn's hair splayed across the pink shirt in a truly appalling color combination that made him wince involuntarily.

Still holding the young woman in her arms, the director looked over Lyn's shoulder at Cal. ''So you're Mr. McCall. I'm Rilla. Your sister is a lovely person.'' She uttered the words in a tone that clearly doubted he shared his sibling's attributes.

He smiled, giving the director, or housemother or whatever the heck she was, his warmest, most sincere smile. It was a smile that had convinced dozens of wary investors to trust him with their hard-earned money, and it didn't fail him this time, either. ''I promise you Miss Hamill will be treated with the utmost respect in my home, ma'am. Is there anything special I can do to make her more comfortable?''

The matron laughed, a full, hearty belly laugh that matched the warm twinkle in her heavily mascaraed eyes. "Other than having a sex-change operation, I doubt there's much you can do to make her more comfortable."

"Sorry. That's not in my plans." Cal grinned as Rilla gave her charge a final squeeze and pushed her toward his waiting truck.

"You go ahead, honey. I want to have a little word with Mr. McCall."

The young woman murmured something in a low voice that he didn't catch, the first sound he'd heard her utter, and returned the woman's hug with a stranglehold that would have been lethal if she'd been any bigger than a twig. Then the two women parted, and Lyn reached for the pathetic paper bag.

"I'll get that." Cal moved toward her. It couldn't be too heavy but he'd bet his last dime she'd struggle to drag it to the truck. He reached out for the bag she was about to pick up, and the girl gave a panicked squeak. Cal stepped back involuntarily, and Lyn backed away from him so fast she fetched up hard against the lady still standing behind her.

"Honey, honey," the woman soothed. "It's all right. Mr. McCall's a *gentleman*. He's only going to carry the bag for you." She patted Lyn's shoulder and gave her a gentle push. "You go get in the truck now."

There was a brief silence while Lyn took a deep, shaky breath that he could hear clear over where he waited, then walked off. Cal shook his head, pushing his hat back and hooking his thumbs in the pockets of his jeans, rocking back on his heels in thought. This was looking worse and worse. How was he going to deal with a housekeeper who was terrified of him? "I'm not so sure this is going to work out," he said to Rilla.

"Well, I'm not sure it's going to work, either," the big woman informed him, hands on hips. "Your sister thinks you're a saint. But frankly, I'm not so sure you're up to the task of dealing with a little wounded critter like that." She pointed to his truck where Lyn was sitting obediently.

That stung. It was one thing for *him* to say it wouldn't work, but he'd be damned if he'd let somebody else judge him and find him lacking.

"I can deal with her," he said, injecting confidence into his tone. "I just don't want to scare her any more than she already is."

Rilla sighed. "She's got to get used to being around men again. Your sister gave me some references on you and everybody I talked to says you're a good man."

He was astounded, then outraged. "You called people for character references on me?"

The woman shrugged, but her eyes were filled with glee. "You bet. I have to be sure my clients are going to be safe when they leave here." Then the laughter faded from her eyes and a profound sorrow replaced it. "Mr. McCall, you can't imagine the things I've seen. The things some of the women who come through here have endured. For some of them, simply surviving is a victory. Little Lynnie there, she's got good reason to fear men. I saw her right after your sister brought her to the hospital and I know the doctors weren't real sure she'd ever be the same again. Physically or in her head." She paused, then raised her eyebrows. "She says she doesn't remember anything about what happened. She might never. The important thing is that she have a good, quiet place to recover."

"Is there anything special I should do for her?" He didn't have time for this, he told himself even as the words came out of his mouth. He had a ranch to get back on its feet, stock to buy, men to hire. He didn't have time to baby-sit.

Rilla shook her head. "She doesn't need medical treatment, just time to heal in her heart. You be gentle, give her lots of space, and time'll do the rest. She's got a support group that meets here if she needs it. I'll call her once in a while and see how she's doing. Your sister said she'd check on Lynnie occasionally."

Cal nodded, trying to suppress the smile that threatened at the mention of his sister. He knew that to Silver "occasionally" probably meant two or three times a day. "She's due back from her honeymoon in a few days and I imagine she'll be over to make sure everything's going okay." He took a deep breath. "Well, Miss Rilla, you come visit anytime you like. We'll feed you and there are plenty of empty bedrooms for a guest."

"Thank you." The woman put out her hand, and when he took it, she gave his hand a heftier shake than many of the ranchers he knew were capable of. "You take care of Lynnie and call if you have any questions." She reached out and tucked a piece of paper in his shirt pocket. "There's my number. Any time of the night or day. Emergencies don't keep business hours."

That sobered him. He knew all about emergencies. "Yes, ma'am," he said. "We'll hope that little gal has had all the emergencies she's going to for one lifetime."

The hour-and-a-half drive home from Rapid City never had seemed so long. His new housekeeper sat silently in her seat, apparently unaware that common courtesy might direct her to make some small effort at conversation.

His thoughts were a jumbled mess and because he was preoccupied with sorting them into order, he didn't bother to try to draw her out. When they reached the town of Wall, he asked her if she needed to stop for anything, but she shook her head. He hoped that meant she wasn't going to need a bathroom for a while because Kadoka, their destination and the next outpost of civilization along this strip of I-90, was another hour away.

When they got off the interstate at Kadoka, he asked her again if she needed to stop, and again she shook her head, so he headed down Route 73 south of town, toward his outfit, and finally, *finally,* he reached the turnoff to his ranch. His ranch. The notion gave him a rush of pleasure every time it occurred to him that he owned the land. He avoided the worst of the ruts in the lane, promising himself that would be one of the next things he'd see to now that he was back for good.

As they came within sight of the house, he couldn't help glancing over at his new employee, wanting to see her reaction to his home place.

Tears were streaming down her face.

He was so shocked he slammed on the brake, jolting them both forward against their seat belts. Lyn shrieked and he immediately cut the engine, saying, "Hey, there, it's all right. It's all right."

She took a trembling breath as he ripped off his hat and raked a hand through his hair. When he could trust his voice to be calm again, he asked, "Have I done something to upset you?"

She shook her head, the red hair flying around her shoulders, but she still, as far as he could tell, hadn't looked directly at him.

"Then why are you crying?" He couldn't keep the trace of exasperation from his voice.

Lyn raised her head. Slowly, she turned to look at him and for the first time, he got to see what she looked like under all that hair. Her eyes were green. No, that was wrong. Her eyes were huge, emerald pools. Unfortunately, around those striking eyes were green and yellow bruises, and a deeper yellow lump stood out on her forehead. Her skin was fair, except for the faint shadows of bruises mottling her face and neck, and she had a faint sprinkling of freckles across her nose and over her cheeks. But it was her mouth that drew his notice.

A long, ugly wound marred the otherwise flawless lower half of a pair of lips that formed a pretty Cupid's bow. The scar came from beneath her jaw on the left side and reached up to claw through her lip. Red marks indicated that stitches had recently been removed, and he suspected that plastic surgery had been done, because the repair looked neat and efficient and already seemed to be fading from what he was sure had been a doozy of a cut.

He was afraid she'd see him staring, so he quickly looked back at her eyes, willing himself to ignore the obvious evidence of damage to her face. Her eyelashes and eyebrows were a rich dark chestnut, the brows arching elegantly above those unforgettable eyes.

Eyes that were still sparkling with tears, he suddenly realized.

Again, he said, "Why are you crying?"

She opened her mouth. Worked it, but no sound came out. Again she tried, and this time a trickle of a husky whisper reached his ears. "I used to live here."

One

Nine weeks later...

Lyn Hamill glanced at the sturdy waterproof watch on her left wrist. It wasn't exciting, as jewelry went, but she treasured it because Cal McCall had given it to her the second week after she'd come to work at his ranch. Almost four o'clock. Good. She used the back of her arm to wipe sweat from her forehead and grabbed the tongs, deftly plucking the canning jars from the boiling water and replacing them with another batch while the first ones cooled. She would have enough time to finish the last half-bushel of tomatoes before her employer came in for dinner.

Carrying a load of completely cooled tomato jars to the basement, she took a moment to survey her handiwork with a feeling of satisfaction. Although she had

arrived at the ranch in July, too late for any planting, she
had managed to get a good start on stocking up for winter. Now, onions and garlic hung from the wooden rafters
in net bags and bushel baskets of potatoes stood on the
bare dirt floor. She was steadily filling the wooden
shelves that stood against three walls. Already they held
canning jars filled with bread-and-butter pickles, green
beans, peas, plum butter, buffaloberry jelly and the tomatoes she was putting up today.

Cal gave her a household allowance from which she
was to buy groceries and anything else she thought they
needed. She was a frugal shopper and the allowance was
generous, so she'd bought vegetables to replace the
things she would have planted if she'd been here in the
spring. Neighbors had given her the tomatoes and a number of other things. Or more accurately, they'd given Cal
gifts to welcome him back to the community and she'd
been the logical recipient, since he was out on the range
most of the time.

She'd helped Cal's sister dig the potatoes, and Silver
had insisted she take some home. And just yesterday
she'd harvested some squash that had come up by itself
and managed to survive all summer unattended. It was
September now and she'd been home—here—nearly nine
weeks. *It's not your home anymore,* she reminded herself
sternly. She was merely an employee of the owner. And
as such, she'd pick apples tomorrow and make pies with
the little red ones. The others would make good applesauce and apple butter.

Upstairs, a door slammed. Her hand flew to her throat
and her body jolted. Her breathing stuttered, and for a
moment, she could hear her heartbeat roaring in her ears.
Fear froze her feet to the floor.

He'd finally found her. If she'd still been holding the

tomato jars, they'd be shattered on the sod floor. *Wayne.* God, what was she going to do? She was trapped down here. What if he—what? What if he *what?* Just as she had each time she tried to recall the events of the last months, she drew a blank. Oh, if only she could remember!

"Lyn? Where's the peroxide?"

Cal. Relief swept through her and she consciously relaxed all the muscles that had tensed in subconscious dread—*of what?* She took a deep, calming breath. It was only Cal.

Turning, she hurried up the steps and into the kitchen.

Her employer stood before the sink and as she reached his side, she saw blood dripping from a cut along one finger. Quickly, she got the peroxide from the cupboard where she'd organized all the first aid supplies and held it out to him, noticing as she did so that her hands were shaking visibly, a remnant of her fear. Then she realized he wouldn't be able to unscrew the cap easily so she did it for him, moving to his side and tilting the bottle over the injured finger.

Cal hissed in a breath between his teeth as the cleanser washed away the blood and bubbled dirt to the surface of the wound. She hated hurting him but there was no help for it. Gently, she slipped her hand beneath his and angled the finger up, pouring more peroxide over the torn flesh. And as she concentrated on the small task, the stomach-knotting sense of panic inside her faded, to be replaced with another feeling.

Cal's steely arm was pressed against her shoulder and she shivered with pleasure at their proximity. He treated her casually, in a friendly offhand manner, and there were very few times when she'd been this close to him. There were even fewer times when she'd actually touched him.

Her fingers trembled beneath his and Cal made an abrupt motion, taking the bottle from her and stepping a pace away. "Thanks," he said. "I can do it."

She was so disappointed by his dismissal she could have cried. Turning away, she went to the stove and checked the timer, then took the next batch of canning jars from the water.

"Tomatoes." Cal's voice sounded hopeful. "Maybe you could make some spaghetti sauce with a few of those this winter."

She nodded, unable to keep her face from lighting up. Mentally, she made another note in her "Special Things To Do For Cal" file. Forgetting anything that might make Cal McCall's life more comfortable or enjoyable was unacceptable to her. He'd given her back so much that she could never repay him. This was her small way of letting him know she appreciated it.

She extended the same appreciation to Cal's sister, Silver, and her husband, Deck. They'd helped her when she didn't know anyone in the world could help her, and her small gifts of special foodstuffs, recipes and handmade clothing was her way of saying thank-you.

Although it wasn't strictly true that she felt the same way about them as she did about Cal. No, the way she felt about Cal was unique. There might be things she couldn't remember, would never remember, but she knew she'd never felt before the way she felt about the man who owned the ranch where she'd lived once. Certainly she'd never felt about her ex-husband as she did about Cal.

She sneaked a glance sideways at him, still standing at the sink. He hadn't taken off his summer straw hat. He rarely did, until he was ready to take a shower in the evening after working all day, but it didn't matter to her.

His hat was such a part of him that he almost looked naked without it.

It was still terribly hot during the day, and he wore a lightweight long-sleeved shirt that clung to his broad shoulders. He'd been riding, she knew, because she could see the horse tethered just outside the yard, and a dark stain of sweat dampened the back center of the shirt from his neck down to where it vanished beneath his jeans.

His jeans. Oh, she loved the way those pants fit him. She could still remember the first time she'd noticed the way the fabric molded his tight, lean buttocks. She'd been at the ranch for three days, three days in which Cal had insisted she take her time getting to know the place and settling in. He wouldn't even let her cook at first, until the morning of that third day when she'd gotten up earlier than he had.

She'd gone into the kitchen and made him a hearty breakfast of biscuits and gravy. She'd also made him a lunch to take along since he'd mentioned he'd be haying again all day. Cal had come into the kitchen just as she had finished, sniffing the air appreciatively.

She'd handed him a mug of coffee. He'd sampled it and said, "You're hired!" Then he'd walked over to the door to get his boots, which she'd cleaned up the night before. As he bent, the denim pulled taut across the back of his strong thighs, drawing her eyes and drying her mouth in a manner that surprised and shocked her so much she'd turned away and shoveled his breakfast onto a plate.

She could almost giggle at the memory now.

She had to walk to the sink, where he was still standing, with a pitcher she filled from the sink, and as she did so, she took a moment to peer at the cut. It wasn't such a bad one that it would need stitches, but a bandage and some antibiotic ointment certainly were in order. Quickly, she added the water to the pot that was boiling on the stove, filling the room with clouds of steam and the smell of hot tomato.

Then she went to the cupboard again as Cal dried the cut with a paper towel. Taking down the things she needed, she approached him, holding them out before her and looking at him in question.

"Yeah," he said, nodding. "I guess I'd better put something on it. The wire snapped and I ducked, but it caught me there on the way by."

She shuddered. He'd been repairing fence and she winced at the thought of what a piece of barbed wire could do when it suddenly was severed from the tension between the posts.

She set down the box of bandages and tore one open, then added some of the antibiotic cream to the center before taking his hand in hers again. He extended the finger and she carefully positioned the gauze, wrapping it securely with tape and neatly trimming the ends. Her hands were trembling at the feel of his hard, callused flesh against hers. At night, her dreams were filled with those hands and the magic she imagined they could work on her body.

But those were only dreams. Standing here, holding his hand in the kitchen, was *real* and being close to him was sweet torture. His broad chest loomed before her, making her feel small and feminine, though she'd never been short in her entire life. Beanpole, the boys at school had called her.

She looked at him and smiled. "There," she said. "I think you'll live."

Cal gazed down at her from his superior height, warmth in his gray eyes. "That's the first joke I've ever heard you make,'' he said. This close, she could see the black rim around the irises, the tiny flecks of black that fractured the silver throughout, the dark fringe of his lashes and the strong slash of his black brows that nearly met in the center. He smiled, holding her gaze with his. ''You've come a long way since the day I brought you here,'' he said.

She cleared her throat, embarrassed by the praise implied in the comment. ''I'm starting to feel...useful again.''

He nodded, and she knew he understood what she hadn't expressed very well. ''Oh, you're definitely useful,'' he said in a teasing tone. ''I don't know how this place got by until you came along.'' Before she knew it, his hands slid firmly around her shoulders and he pulled her into a close embrace.

She knew an instant of blind, black fear that threatened to engulf her, but as quickly as it enveloped her it vanished. These were Cal's arms and this was Cal's body, and nothing could make her fear him. As the hard length of his big frame registered, she closed her eyes and inhaled his scent—not difficult since her nose was buried in his chest. He smelled of saddle leather and horse, of hay and healthy man sweat and some other, less definable scent that was uniquely his own.

Of all the things she'd expected him to do, this wasn't at the top of the list...she didn't really care as long as he held her like this.

But as fast as the moment had begun, it ended. Releasing her, Cal stepped back. ''Sorry if I scared you,'' he said. ''I appreciate the help.''

She ducked her head and nodded without looking at him, embarrassed again. Had he sensed how badly she longed for him? She would be utterly humiliated if he ever found out how she felt. To cover her awkwardness, she rushed into speech. "You didn't scare me. You caught me by surprise for a moment, that's all."

Cal's eyebrows rose. He grinned then, and her heart skipped a beat at the devilish gleam in his dark gray eyes. "I was beginning to wonder if you spoke more than one sentence at a time."

"I can talk," she said defensively. "I just haven't had much to say." Her voice sounded loud to her own ears, and huskier than she remembered. The doctor had said there might be permanent damage to her vocal cords from the attempt to strangle her. She didn't guess it mattered— she'd never been much of a singer and as long as she could communicate, it didn't really matter how she sounded.

Cal stood perfectly still, staring at her with a strange expression on his face. When the silence stretched on, she finally said, "What?"

He shrugged and smiled at her, breaking the odd tension of the moment. "Your voice is really husky. Has it always been like that?"

"It's different," she said. "I don't sound like me anymore."

He nodded. "Give it a few more months. It hasn't been used in a while. Maybe you just need to get used to talking on a regular basis again."

She nodded.

Silence.

"Well, I've got to get back out there and finish that fence," he said. "Wilson's new bull's been in the pasture over by the dam three times this week. If he tears the fence down again, I swear I'm going to butcher him and deliver the meat to Wilson."

She smiled as he headed out the door. Containing your

cattle and keeping your neighbor's out was an unending chore on a ranch, and for all his fierce talk she had learned that Cal was a good neighbor.

He mounted Tor, his big bay gelding, and she watched from the window as he and the horse disappeared over the ridge that led to the dam pasture. When the top of his hat had completely vanished behind the ridge, she turned back to her tomatoes. Yes, she'd have to make a couple big batches of spaghetti sauce this winter. She knew Silver had recipes for things like lasagna and stuffed shells. Maybe she'd share them.

Lyn always was conscious of the fact that Cal was a cosmopolitan man. He'd eaten fancy foods in New York that she'd never even heard of and though he praised her cooking and told her he'd missed ranch life and plain, hearty ranch fare, she worried that she wouldn't do a good job for him.

Man, did he ever hate haying.

Cal itched all over. The seeds from the alfalfa had gotten into every crevice, every orifice, every pore. For the last two hours of the day, he fantasized about jumping in the stock pond, imagining the cool water sluicing over him, cleansing his skin of the prickly, dry hay.

The thought reminded him of a time in New York when he'd still been pretending he enjoyed wearing a suit and tie, a time he'd taken his girl of the moment out to a deserted reservoir and the two of them had gone skinny-dipping. And *that* thought brought to mind another, entirely inappropriate fantasy, one too close to home.

In his daydreaming, Lyn was riding with him. When they reached the stock pond, they dismounted and disrobed. He watched, pulse pounding and body stirring, as she pulled off her boots and stepped out of her jeans, then slowly, teasingly, unbuttoned her shirt one button at a time until the garment hung loosely around her, an open strip down the center showing him that beneath the practical work clothes she'd worn no undergarments of any kind.

He walked toward her and pushed the shirt off her shoulders, then turned her toward the pond, and together they took the few steps to the edge of the cool water. They waded in and as the water reached his waist, then his chest, he drew her into his arms, feeling her slippery curves against him....

He groaned as he dismounted and put away the horse. He must be nuts, torturing himself like this. Lyn was his employee. In no way had she given him any reason to believe she'd welcome a bout of wild sex, in or out of the stock pond. She was a woman who'd been physically abused by someone, probably her ex-husband if the hospital records of her previous injuries were any guide. He'd bet she'd run screaming if she knew of the thoughts slipping into his head with increasing regularity. Hell, she'd gone stiff as a board when he'd given in to that stupid impulse in the kitchen yesterday and grabbed her. His only excuse was that she made him forget good sense when she was around. He snorted. Some excuse. He'd even noticed her hands shaking with fear when she'd been close to his side doctoring his cut and still he'd hugged her to him without a thought as to how it might affect her.

He stomped to the house, thoroughly annoyed with himself. Why in hell couldn't he stop thinking about her?

It must be the proximity thing, he decided. She'd been living in his home for over two months now, sleeping in a bedroom just steps away, making his meals, washing his clothes, helping with anything he asked. She never complained, no matter what he asked of her.

Of course, until yesterday she hadn't spoken to him except for the barest, briefest possible responses, so he didn't really know for sure that she wasn't the whiny type.

But deep inside, he did know.

According to his sister's husband, who had lived here in Jackson County all his life, Lyn was raised around Belvidere, the next little town to the east. Cal had spent his childhood in the county, but he didn't recall ever knowing who she was. Of course, she'd have been five or six years younger than he was, anyway. Her mother had died when she was small and her daddy had never married again. Lyn was a quiet little thing who had worked with her father and took care of his house. People remembered she was a good cook, something he'd already learned.

But other than that, nobody remembered much. Her daddy had leased ranch land from the Pine Ridge Indian Reservation, and after Cal's father had died the same year that Cal had started college back East, apparently Hamill had bought his property. Lyn would have been a young teenager, he figured, if her daddy had bought it then.

He should remember her, but he didn't. Cal honestly couldn't remember much about that time. After an accident at the end of his senior year of high school in which his friend Genie had died, he hadn't been able to get out of town fast enough. And he'd been gone less than six months when his father had suffered a fatal heart attack and died and the ranch had been sold to Lyn's father.

With an effort, he shook off the past. Though he'd always regret those lost last months with his father, he'd come to terms with Genie's death, as had her family. Her brother Deck and he had repaired the hard feelings between them. He was home again, in more ways than one.

But his home needed work. A lot of work. Hamill hadn't been much of a rancher, according to Deck. He'd only worked the outfit for three years before he died and the ranch was bought by a guy from up near Philip who hadn't done much with it, either. He'd had it until he retired and moved up to Sturgis.

And that's when Cal had bought the land that had once been his father's. When he'd heard the asking price, he'd been shocked. When had dusty-dry sod in the Badlands gotten so expensive? He'd decided it was a good thing he'd worked on the New York Stock Exchange and made a small killing in the process. He'd need it to start up a ranch from scratch.

His thoughts circled back to Lyn...nobody remembered anything much after her daddy passed away and the ranch changed hands. They thought she'd married. The couple had drifted over to Rapid, someone thought. But nobody had seen her in a while, which was unusual enough in western South Dakota to raise eyebrows. *Wonder where that Hamill girl went off to?* The area was so sparsely populated that the locals joked that they knew everyone in the whole damned state.

He stopped in the mudroom that he'd added on recently and peeled off his boots. He carried both his shirt and his undershirt in his hand; he'd taken them off outside the door, shaken them out and used them to dust himself down. Tossing them into the washing machine, he moved into the adjacent bathroom to shower off the rest of the day's grime. When he was finished, he grabbed one of the big bath sheets his sister Silver had bought when she redecorated his home, wrapping it around his waist. He'd seen Lyn outside firing up the barbecue grill when he'd come in, so he strode through the house in nothing but his towel. God, it felt good to get that scratchy seed off him.

Padding up the stairs, he walked down the hall to his bedroom. Every time he walked through the house, he felt more and more satisfied at the changes that had been made. And still were being made. He'd hired carpenters to repair some of the woodwork and sagging doors right after he'd bought the place. Then Silver had hired painters and wallpaperers and she'd gone through and spruced the place up with her own little touches, adding stenciling, rugs and window treatments. He'd been called out of town while she was still working on it and when he'd gotten home, she'd practically finished redecorating. Good thing, too, since she'd decided to marry Deck only weeks later. Now she was busy designing their own home while she got ready for the baby that would arrive near Valentine's Day.

His bedroom door was ajar and he pushed it wide as he walked into the room.

Lyn whirled at his entrance, one hand going to her throat where she stood in front of his dresser putting away stacks of clothing. She didn't make a sound, but her face went so completely white she scared him.

"Whoa, sorry," he said. "I didn't mean to scare you. I thought you were outside."

"I—I wasn't."

He nearly smiled but she still looked too rattled. "I can see that." He waited, but she didn't move a muscle. Finally, he cleared his throat. "Um, how about you finding some other chore to do while I get dressed?"

"Oh!" The color flooded back into her cheeks and she flushed a deep scarlet in keeping with her vibrant hair. "I'm sorry. I'll just—I'll just get out now." She scurried past him, head down, edging sideways so as not to touch him, and vanished down the hallway before he could say another word.

Cal shook his head ruefully as he closed the bedroom door. Dropping the towel, he stood naked, hands on his hips while the cool air circulated by the ceiling fan he'd had installed washed over him. Poor thing. He'd seen some of the evidence of what had been done to her, and he'd heard more. Her ex-husband must have been a pathetic excuse for a man. No real man would hit a female much less beat her the way Lyn had been beaten. He felt a flicker of bone-deep rage at the thought of the bruises that she'd still borne when he'd first brought her to the ranch. That beautiful skin should never have known a bruise.

Her skin was so fair and milky-white that it was practically translucent, and he'd found himself fascinated by the parade of tiny freckles that marched across her nose. Every time he was near her, he had to hold in check the urge to reach out and trace them with a fingertip. She had a light scattering of freckles over her arms, as well, and he wondered if there were any other parts of her that were freckled.

Then he grimly shook his head, looking down the length of his body, which had responded instantly to thoughts of Lyn. He was a first-class jerk, lusting after a skinny little female who'd been manhandled like she had been. This was getting ridiculous. He needed a woman. He'd been too busy in New York those last few months to bother dating much, and he'd been celibate since he'd moved home. No wonder he was fantasizing about his housekeeper.

Maybe it was time to start thinking about looking for a wife. Even before the last couple hectic months, when he'd been busy transferring all his hard-won clients to other brokers he trusted and hammering out the buying arrangements for the ranch, he hadn't minded his single state. Most of the time he'd been too tired by the end of a wild day on Wall Street and when he had wanted feminine companionship, he'd availed himself of the multitudes of liberated single career women who didn't want attachments any more than he had. But now...now things were different. Now he could devote time to a family if he started one. As he dressed and started down the stairs, the word stuck in his head, replaying over and over. *Family...family...family...* He was determined to have a family of his own some day, a real family, with both parents in the household and a bunch of kids running around—nothing like the rather lonely existence he'd known growing up. Though his father had loved him, he'd keenly felt the difference between what he'd always thought of as "real" families and his own.

His annual summer visits with his mother in Virginia only reinforced the loneliness. He was the outsider. His mother, her second husband and Silver, his half sister, were a happy, tight-knit trio. He'd always wondered if his own life would have been like that if his mother hadn't abandoned his father and him.

Lyn had supper ready when he walked into the kitchen, and he sniffed the air with interest. "What do I smell?"

She turned from the stove, where she was transferring a pot of steaming broccoli to a serving dish. "Marinated pork chops. It's not fancy." Was it his imagination or did she sound faintly defensive?

"I don't care how un-fancy it is," he assured her. "It smells fantastic."

And it was, as were the homemade muffins, the stewed apples and the devils' food cake she set before him when the table had been cleared. It was just the two of them, since the men who worked for him had families of their own and went home at the end of the day. He'd gotten into the habit early on of telling her all about his day, mostly as a way of filling the silence at the table. Tonight was no different except that she asked questions a few times instead of nodding and raising an eyebrow to get him to continue.

She grimaced when he told her about the young rabbit that had gotten caught in the sickle. "I know it's impossible to miss them, but it always made me cry," she said.

Cal nodded. "Well, I did manage to avoid hitting a fawn today. You should have seen him run."

Her eyes glowed, a striking emerald in the evening light coming through the big window by the nook where the kitchen table was set, and he was reminded of cats' eyes in the dark. "They're so sweet when they're little," she said. Then she chuckled. "Of course, I even think calves are sweet, so I guess my judgment is suspect."

Cal smiled at that. "God, I missed this life. I didn't even realize how much until I got back again. I can't wait for calving season."

Her eyebrows rose in that silent way of hers. "You have to get through winter first," she reminded him.

"Don't I know it," he grumbled. "It's going to be a long one." He rose from the table then, picking up his plate to take it to the dishwasher.

"Oh, don't. I'll do that." Lyn rushed over and whisked the plate from his hand, along with the water glass and fork he'd lifted.

"I don't mind. You work hard enough during the day," he said.

"But *I* mind," she said. "You work hard, too, and this is what you're paying me for." She crossed to the dishwasher and rinsed the plate before setting it in the rack.

"I haven't told you how much I appreciate you giving me this chance," she said slowly.

"You don't have to. I promised Silver I'd hire you but I also told her I couldn't keep you on if you didn't work out. I need someone I can depend on to be in charge of the house." He gazed across the kitchen at her. "I can depend on you. The job is yours as long as you want it."

She stared at him, and to his dismay her eyes filled with tears. "Thank you," she whispered.

He shrugged, uncomfortable with her gratitude. "No big deal." And before she could really get the water-works flowing, he beat a hasty retreat to the living room to catch the evening news. But as he sat, trying to focus on what was happening in the rest of the world, he was far too conscious of the woman moving around in the kitchen. When she finally turned out the kitchen light, his body relaxed in relief as she started for the stairs.

"Good night," she said.

"Good night." Now he wished he could get her to sit down and talk some more. He was fascinated by her husky, musical voice. That voice smacked of long after-noons making love in dim bedrooms and every time she spoke, his body reacted to the promise in those sexy tones. Just yesterday, when she'd been helping him bandage his finger, that voice had distracted him into an erotic dream. Then her whole face had lit up when he'd told her she seemed like she was getting better, and he hadn't been able to resist hugging her. The feel of her warm, firm frame against his—

And this was ridiculous! Here he was again, in a hot sweat having totally inappropriate dreams about his housekeeper. He practically leaped out of the chair and grabbed the phone off the kitchen wall, rapidly punching the buttons.

Deck answered on the third ring. "What?" The single word was a snarl.

"Well, that's a heck of a way to greet your brother-in-law."

"You're interrupting us. What do you want?" Deck sounded distinctly disgruntled and Cal realized exactly what he'd interrupted. He grimaced. Was everybody in the world getting next to a warm body except for him?

"A woman."

"Then go find one." The receiver clicked off decisively on the other end.

Cal sighed. Lifting the phone again, he punched in Deck's brother Marty's telephone number. He hit the speakerphone as he ambled across the kitchen and yanked open the refrigerator door, surveying its contents. As his best buddy's voice came on the other end of the line, he selected a soda.

"Lucky Stryke."

"Hey, neighbor. Is your kid in bed?"

"Yeah. Thank God." Marty's answer sounded heartfelt and Cal grinned. He'd been around Marty's daughter, Cheyenne, a number of times since his move back out here, and she was...unforgettable. A stunning little beauty who looked like her dead mother and acted—unfortunately—a lot like her deceased aunt Genie, who'd been a hell-raiser from the day she was born until the day she died young in the accident that was reason he'd left South Dakota all those years ago.

"What are you up to?" Marty's voice called him back from the past.

He popped the top on his soda and leaned against the counter. "Where the heck do you go when you want to meet women out here?"

A low rumble of laughter vibrated through the connection. "A bar."

"That's not the kind of woman I want to meet," Cal said.

"Oh, hell."

"What's that supposed to mean?"

"You're starting to sound like me. You got marriage on your mind?"

"No, I do *not* have marriage on my mind." He conveniently ignored the fact that he'd been thinking that very thing only hours ago. "I just need to get laid. And I'd prefer to do it with somebody I like and enjoy spending time with."

Something moving in the corner of his vision made him whip his head around. Though he saw nothing, he'd have sworn he saw a shadow in the kitchen doorway just for an instant. He moved toward the door, but realized he couldn't leave the room without picking up the handset of the phone. Shrugging, he turned his attention to what Marty was saying.

"…know what you mean. I'm meeting a girl at the city bar tomorrow night. She, uh, answered my ad."

Cal laughed aloud. He'd heard about Marty's other disastrous encounters that were a result of advertising in the personals for a wife. To his way of thinking, the guy was insane. "I might have to check this out. What time?"

"Eight. I figure if she's willing to meet me in a bar, she can't be a teetotaler who thinks I'll go to hell if I drink a beer."

"That's logical. Eight, huh? You might see me."

"Sounds good. You can rescue me if this date turns out to be a bust." His oldest friend's voice sounded hopeful.

Cal stifled a comment about the odds of that being pretty good. "It's a deal."

Two

He raked the mown hay with two of his men the next day and came in grumpy and sweaty with broken blisters on the hand where he'd held the dump rope. He'd bought the machinery along with the ranch and it didn't look like one damn thing had been added since his father's time. He promised himself the next time he got a chance to look around, he'd buy a swather that would mow and rake at the same time. Then he'd have a ceremonial burning of the old hay rake.

The house smelled of something wonderful again—a roast in the oven—and by the time he'd showered and changed, he felt marginally more human. When he came back down, Lyn was flitting around the kitchen getting the roast, potatoes and carrots out of the pan, and he picked up a pot holder and pulled the rolls from the second oven. As he did, he watched her from the corner of his eye.

She wore a simple blue T-shirt the same color as her jeans with the boots he'd bought her at the end of her first week on the ranch. They were scuffed and marked already, since she insisted on helping around the barn and pastures when she wasn't working in the house, though he noticed she was careful to keep them clean and waterproofed.

As she stretched for a meat fork in a far drawer, the T-shirt drew taut against her slender body, profiling the gentle rise of plump, rounded breasts. She'd gained some weight in the time she'd been at the ranch and oh, mama, it had all gone to the right places. His pulse changed to a faster rhythm and his body began to react, and he hastily grabbed a basket for the rolls and took a seat at the table before she noticed he had a hard-on the size of Mount Rushmore. Damn, but he was tired of feeling like this. It was a good thing he was going to town tonight.

Maybe he'd just drive right on to Rapid after he met Marty. He'd met a widowed gal there a month ago when he'd gone to the airport to pick up Deck and Silver. She'd been waiting for her mother on the same flight and they'd struck up a conversation. She'd made it plain she'd have welcomed his call after that and he wondered if she'd go out with him on short notice.

But at the table a few minutes later, thoughts of the Rapid City widow vanished. An idea occurred to him as he watched Lyn slip into her seat across from his with the unassuming air of someone who didn't expect to be noticed. "Go to town with me tonight."

The notion clearly startled her. "Me? Oh, no thank y—"

"It wasn't a request," he informed her. "It was an order from the boss."

Her green eyes widened. "But why? I don't want to

go to town. There's nothing open on Friday night but the bars—''

"Which is where we're going. I have to meet Marty there at eight. You need to start getting out of the house. This will be a good way to begin.''

She wore a sulky pout that thrust out her lower lip in an adorable expression that made him want to lean across the table and put his mouth on hers. "I don't like bars,'' she muttered, though he noticed she didn't tell him no.

He supposed she had good reason for not liking bars. Her father had been a drunk, and his poor ranching probably had been a direct result of his fondness for the bottle. And judging from what he'd heard of her marital history from his sister's snooping into police files and hospital records, he suspected the husband who'd hammered on her also had an alcohol problem.

"I'll drink soda,'' he told her. "You won't have to worry about pouring me into the truck for the drive home.''

The pout eased from her face and he didn't know whether to be glad or sorry. He was an idiot, asking her to go to town with him when *she* was what he wanted to get away from. But he'd realized she hadn't been off the ranch a single time since she'd arrived except to venture down to Silver's house or to buy groceries. And it was past time she stopped hiding herself away. Women out here needed companionship, other women, to talk to— he was convinced that had been half the reason his mother had packed up and left when he was a baby. She'd refused to make friends with the "locals,'' as she'd called them, according to his father, and the loneliness had gotten to her.

Lyn met him in the kitchen half an hour later. She had exchanged the blue T-shirt for a pretty blouse with long, full sleeves and she'd taken her hair out of the thick braid she usually wore it in when she was working. Wild curls quirked around her face and cascaded over her shoulders and as she came into the room she shoved it behind one ear with an impatient gesture. "I'm ready."

His stomach muscles clenched. It was an effort to pull himself together. "All right. Let's go." His fingers itched to plunge into those curls, to drag her against him and unbutton each and every one of the pretty little pearl buttons that marched down the front of the blouse. He wiped a drop of sweat from his temple. He had to get over this.

They walked into the city bar a quarter-hour later to find Marty already seated in one of the red vinyl booths with a woman. It took a few minutes to get to the table because people at each of the three booths before Marty's and at the bar had to come over and welcome Lyn back. Finally, sensing she was a bit overwhelmed, Cal put a hand beneath her elbow. "Come on over here," he said. "We have to check out Marty's newest applicant."

"Applicant?" Her eyebrows rose.

"For the job he advertised. He put an ad in the personals for a wife," he explained, enjoying the look of incredulity that flashed across her mobile features.

"You're teasing me."

"Nope." He solemnly placed his hand over his heart. "Swear to God it's the truth."

By that time they were at the table. Marty had been seated across from his date and when he saw them coming, he stood and waved.

"Hi, Lynnie," he said. "Hey, Cal. I'd like you to meet Iris."

Iris was a stunning brunette with enormous brown eyes and jugs the size of watermelons straining at the front of a bright yellow sweater. Though the sweater wasn't exceptionally tight or low-cut, Cal had a hard time meeting her eyes.

"Hello," Iris said, smiling at them.

Lyn slid into the booth and Cal tipped his hat to the woman before lowering himself onto the seat beside Lyn. Marty had a smug smile on his face. "Iris is a jewelry designer," he told them. "She does pieces in Black Hills gold."

"That's interesting." Lyn surprised him when she spoke up. "I've always loved that look. Did you design your earrings?"

"Yes." Iris and Marty both had beers in front of them and she took a pull at her bottle before answering Lyn's questions about her work. The conversation was steady as Iris, in turn, asked questions about ranching, and Cal could almost see Marty sizing up her ring finger. Among other things.

This one seemed cultured, intelligent, sexy...he couldn't believe a woman like this resorted to answering personal ads. There *had* to be some catch.

After three hours, he knew what it was. Iris drank like a fish.

Lyn, to her credit, made a valiant effort to prevent a disaster. She carried on a conversation about jewelry design with the woman until the subject was wrung dry. When it became apparent that Iris could talk and drink at the speed of light, Lyn asked for a pizza and some chips for their table. Cal flashed her a grin, knowing she was hoping the food would soak up some of the alcohol.

The evening wore on. Marty's smug smile had long since glazed over into stupefied horror as his dream woman deteriorated into a giddy, slurring nightmare. She shrieked with laughter at things that weren't funny. She excused herself at least ten times to go to the bathroom and each time, she got into a cozy conversation with the cowboys parked at the bar.

By eleven, Marty was slumped in his seat, shaking his head in embarrassment. "What am I going to do now?" he moaned. "I can't let her drive back to Rapid in that condition. And I'm sure as hell not taking her back to the ranch!"

Cal was doubled over with laughter and even Lyn was giggling helplessly as they watched Iris climb into the lap of a cowboy barely old enough to be in the bar in the first place.

Marty regarded them with a sour expression. "Oh, sure, go ahead and laugh. Just don't ever come to me for help when you guys have trouble with romance."

"It really isn't funny," Lyn said, her tone sobering. "That girl's got problems."

"And so do I," said Marty.

Cal sighed, wiping his eyes on a napkin. He felt magnanimous, particularly since he couldn't recall ever having a date that was such a disaster. "You two go ahead and leave." He picked up Iris's car keys from the table where they'd lain the whole evening. "Take her car over to the Dakota Inn and then go on home. I'll tell her you had an emergency and had to leave, Marty, and I'll take her over there and get her a room."

The grateful look on Marty's face was nearly enough to set him off again. He didn't dare look at Lyn as she said, "Sounds like a plan." He slid out of the booth and let her out, then held her jacket for her and watched her walk out of the bar with Marty. As the pair exited through the glass door, he forced down the envy that tried to rear its head. He'd assumed he'd be the one taking Lyn home tonight.

It was a good ten minutes before he decided that Iris wasn't going to notice Marty's absence, so he strode over and broke up her little party. He was suddenly impatient to get out of the smoky bar.

"Sorry, you're stuck with me," he told the staggering woman. "Marty had to go home." He took her over to the motel and paid for a night's lodging, then showed her to her room and got the heck out of there. Marty and Lyn had driven her car over and parked it outside. Marty's truck was nowhere in sight, and as Cal drove home alone, he told himself it was ridiculous to feel annoyed that Lyn had ridden home with Marty. He'd specifically told her to, hadn't he?

He was a little more than halfway home when the thunderheads that had been threatening for hours unleashed their fury on the Badlands. Instead of the rain everyone had been praying for, hail pelted down from the clouds. Some of the chunks weren't a bad size, but as the wind howled and the storm increased its ferocity, lumps the size of Ping-Pong balls slammed onto the truck and he had to pull off along the side of the road and wait it out. As soon as it abated, he returned to the road and drove home as fast as he dared. He was pretty sure Marty would have dropped Lyn off already and he wondered what she'd do, all alone in the night in a storm like this.

When he pulled the truck to a stop beneath the big pole light in the yard, he could see the dents in the hood from inside the truck. Lyn came out the door before the truck stopped and came down the walk to meet him, and he forced himself to act as unconcerned as she seemed to be. Then she said quietly, "I'm glad you're back. I was worried."

"You okay?"

She nodded.

He walked forward and examined the pits the hail had left on the finish of his pickup, fighting the relief that rushed through his system and feigning a casual attitude. "Oh, well. It looked too new anyway."

Lyn smiled, although he noticed her small face was pale and strained. "Now that's what I call a stretch to find the silver lining." She pointed to the lavender gladiolus that had been in full bloom against the side of the porch, and he could see the strong stalks battered to the ground like fragile grasses. "Darn that hail. In the morning I'll see if any of the glads can be saved as cut flowers. Might as well enjoy them if we can."

He shook his head in admiration as he followed her up the walk and onto the porch. Why had he been worried about her? A lot of women would be upset to tears by the senseless destruction the hail had wrought. But Lyn had grown up here. She knew what to expect and how to handle it when tough things came along.

As he opened the door and motioned for her to precede him into the house, she cast a worried look outside.

"It's so dry," she said. "I was hoping this would be a good rain."

"No such luck." But he was as worried as she. "I'd better spend tomorrow plowing fireguards between the high grass and the east side of the house." With things this hot and dry, fires could spring up from any number of things: stupid tourists flicking cigarettes out the window along the highway, a spark from a train or a piece of machinery or even a lightning strike. Some of the worst fires he'd ever fought growing up out here had been started by lightning.

The next day was as hot as the one before. The daytime temperatures hadn't dropped below eight-five degrees for three weeks and the dry heat was getting to him.

Cal rode toward the house from the west pasture, bringing back four cows and calves he'd sorted out to sell. As he rode, he eyed the brittle grass and the dust that billowed from beneath the cattle's hooves. The horizon rippled and blurred under the baking sun. He'd noticed the waterholes over west were lower than usual.

As he came around the southern end of the ridge, the house came into view. The thrill of being back hadn't worn off yet, and he—

The sheriff's car was bumping along the lane.

The sheriff's car? Mild puzzlement replaced his pleasure. Now why would the sheriff be at his house?

The answer sprang into his head even as the question passed through and he hurried Tor, pushing the cattle past the house and into the big corral, and tied him within reach of the water trough with an apology for making him wait to get rid of the hot saddle.

He strode toward the house. The car was parked in the yard. Had they finally found Lyn's ex-husband? He hoped so. And he sincerely hoped there'd come a day when he could have five minutes alone in a locked room with the bastard.

Five minutes was all it would take to pound him to a pulp and castrate him.

He took off his hat and slapped it against his leg to rid himself of some of the dust, absently noting the wear it was showing. Heck, he'd only had it for a few months. Time to buy a new one and keep this one for some of the nastiest work, like branding.

Opening the door, he stepped inside, enjoying the feel of the cooled air. Lyn wouldn't let him turn the air-conditioning on often, but since mid-August, he'd noticed she hadn't turned it off every time he left the house.

The lawman stood just inside the kitchen door with a

second man in civilian clothes beside him. He turned when he heard the door open. "Hey, there, Cal."

"Joe." They'd gone to high school together, and he'd always liked the guy. "You got some good news for Lyn?"

A choking sound made him look across the kitchen. Lyn stood with her back to the sink. No, he corrected himself, Lyn was backed *against* the sink so tight she could have passed for one of the fixtures.

Her green eyes were wide and shocked-looking and her face was a pasty, ghastly white. He could practically smell fear in the cool kitchen air.

"What's going on here?" His voice was less welcoming and he deliberately allowed a growl to work its way into the words. He didn't know what the sheriff had said to frighten Lyn, but he already knew he didn't like anybody coming into his house without warning and scaring her all to pieces.

Joe Parker cleared his throat, clearly choosing his words carefully. He gestured to the man with him. "This is Detective Biddle from the Pennington County Sheriff's Department Office of Investigations." Then he looked across the kitchen at Lyn. "Lyn Galloway is a suspect in the death of a man. I've come to take her to town to answer some questions."

"You have the wrong woman," Cal said flatly. "My housekeeper's name is Lyn Hamill."

"Her maiden name was Hamill. She was married to Wayne Galloway." He turned to Lyn. "You didn't tell him you had a husband?"

"I knew she had a husband. She's been divorced for over a year." Cal could feel fury bubbling its way to the surface, and he clamped down hard on it, knowing he had to stay focused. "She woke up in the hospital two months ago with no memory of anything in her recent past. She was beaten and there were finger marks around her neck. So you can tell her husband from me that if he's the one who put them there, Cal McCall's going to be looking for him.''

Joe held up a warning hand. ''Don't give me a reason to consider you a suspect, Cal.''

''A suspect in *what?*''

Joe lowered his hand slowly, rubbing the other over a jaw stubbled with golden beard, and Biddle spoke for the first time. His blue eyes were cool and assessing. ''Wayne Galloway's body was found in an apartment building in Rapid City last week. According to the landlord, this woman rented one of the apartments from him for the last year.'' He turned to Lyn. ''How long have you been living here?''

Lyn just stared at him.

''She's been here for about two and a half months,'' Cal said impatiently. ''And before that, she was in a women's shelter in Rapid after she was released from the hospital. I have the names of both places, along with her doctor and the director of the shelter.'' He allowed himself the smallest smile of victory. ''So she couldn't have killed him. She hasn't left the ranch without me or Silver since she got here, and then she hasn't gone any farther than Kadoka.''

Biddle shook his head. ''That isn't going to matter,'' he said coolly. ''Whoever killed Galloway stuffed him into a closet in the basement of the building.'' He paused. ''The tenants have been complaining about an odor and somebody finally got annoyed enough to go hunting the source. Coroner says it looks like he's been there awhile.''

''Jeez.'' The stark recitation shook him, he wasn't going to pretend it hadn't, and he saw Lyn's instinctive recoil from the ugly vision.

"So I have to talk to Mrs. Gal—"

"Don't call me that." It was little more than a hoarse whisper, but both men turned to stare at the fragile-looking woman. Lyn spoke slowly, quietly, to the detective. "I don't think—I'm pretty sure, I mean, that I didn't kill anyone, but I don't know that for sure because I can't remember—"

"Lyn." It was a single syllable but it served to halt the words tumbling from her lips.

She stopped speaking and turned to look at Cal.

"Don't say another word until I call a lawyer." He turned to Joe. "Are you arresting her?"

Joe looked shocked by the suggestion. "Heck, no, Cal, of course not. But she's got to answer—"

"Then I'm asking you to leave. Unless you want to arrest her." He looked at Biddle. "If you want to make an appointment to talk to her, I'll have my attorney call your office."

The sheriff regarded him in baffled frustration. "You're making this a bigger deal than it has to be, Cal."

"I'm asking you to leave," Cal repeated, ignoring the glowering detective. He held out a hand to Lyn. "I need your help in the barn."

As if she were a flimsy iron filing and he the magnet, Lyn lurched across the room and took his outstretched hand in a grip so tight he could feel her fingernails digging into his flesh. He transferred her small palm to his other hand and put his arm around her, leaving the two men to find their own way out as he swept her out of the house and across the yard.

As they walked, he was conscious of the slender body beneath his arm, the way her rounded breasts heaved as

she took deep gasps of air, the way the soft flesh of her
hip brushed his with every step they took. He hated himself for his body's preoccupation with hers, but he was
powerless to do anything about it. He'd been fighting a
losing battle with attraction—and arousal—for weeks.

He'd been unable to ignore her from the very beginning. Though she'd quietly insinuated herself into the
daily routine, taking over the care of the house so quickly
and so well that he was grateful every time he stepped
through the door, he'd been fascinated by her heavy mane
of red curls, her fair skin, the curves she acquired as her
slender body regained some weight.

One day he'd walked into the kitchen while she was
stretching on tiptoe for a vase to arrange some wildflow-
ers she'd brought in. It was back on the shelf just far
enough to be out of her reach.

"I'll get it," he'd said, and without thinking, he had
walked across the kitchen and put a casual hand on her
hip while he'd reached over her head for the vase. The
moment he'd felt her slim, fragile body pressed against
his, the mild arousal he'd been feeling from time to time
had come back tenfold. He'd been so astonished at his
body's bold response that he'd thrust her away from him
and gotten the heck out of the kitchen, too flustered to
talk to her.

His *mind* had been astonished. He'd taken her in as a
favor to his sister, and initially, he'd felt nothing but pity
for the silent waif who scurried around him as if he might
grab for her at any moment. After the first week, she'd
relaxed and settled into her role as his housekeeper and
he'd grown more and more aware of her feminine presence in his home. But he hadn't expected to find himself
fighting an inclination to tear off her jeans and lift her

onto his hard, aching flesh and sate himself with her slender, elfin beauty.

As they passed Tor, Cal reached out with his free hand and snagged the bay's reins and led him along with them. "Gotta get this saddle off him," he told her.

But the instant they were in the shadows inside the barn, he forgot everything but the woman who crumpled to her knees. She would have gone down completely if he hadn't still had his arm around her. Hastily, he dropped Tor's reins and put his other arm around her, holding her to him. He could feel her shaking against him and he cursed Joe Parker until the air turned blue. This was the last thing she needed right now.

He half carried her over to the wooden bench outside the tack room and sat down, pulling her onto his lap. Little whimpering sounds came from her throat and he put a big hand against the back of her head, pressing her against his shoulder. She turned her face into his neck and he could feel wet warmth trickle down inside the collar of his shirt.

She was crying. Now he was *really* furious. She was such a little trooper that nothing normally got to her.

"Shh," he soothed in a deep, crooning voice, rocking her against his chest. "It'll be all right. You know I won't let anything happen to you."

There was no response, but after a few more moments, she took a deep breath and let it shudder out. "I can't believe he's dead," she said in a whisper.

"I'm sorry," he said, though for the life of him he couldn't understand why she'd be grieving. He surely couldn't work up any real sorrow over the slimeball's demise.

She stirred against him. "I don't think I am," she said in an odd, expressionless tone. "He was horrible to me.

Even after we were divorced, I was terrified of him. I think what I am is relieved. Does that make me a terrible person?''

He considered for a moment. ''Nope. It makes you a sensible person.''

There was another silence. He stroked his hands up and down her back, enjoying the feel of the little bumpy ridges of her spine beneath his fingertips, feeling her trembling lessen as she calmed.

''I'm going to call a lawyer as soon as we get back to the house,'' he said.

Her body stilled in his arms. Slowly, she drew away far enough to see his face, and her solemn green eyes were wide and shadowed. ''I can't afford a lawyer,'' she said, her voice even huskier than usual.

''I can.'' His voice rang with grim determination. ''Nobody's putting you in jail for something you didn't do.''

She was silent for a long moment and he could see her agile mind performing all kinds of mental maneuvers. Finally, she looked away. ''You don't know I didn't kill him.''

He took her arms and lightly shook her once. ''Yes, I do.''

Her wide eyes darted back to his.

''You've lived in my house for over two months,'' he reminded her. ''I've watched you with my family and friends and with the stock.'' He deliberately smiled and lightened his tone. ''If you haven't killed that damned sneaky goat by now, I can guarantee you've never hurt anybody else.''

She didn't smile back. ''I wish I were as sure of that as you are.'' One slim hand came up and knocked roughly against her temple. "If only I could remember—"

"Don't," he said in a deep, harsh tone. Cal reached up and snagged her hand, then pulled her against him again, threading a hand through her hair and pushing her face into its previous position in the crook of his neck. "Nobody puts marks on you ever again." The moment the words were uttered, he knew they sounded too intense for the working relationship they'd had. But the adrenaline rush that had swept through him at the sheriff's words was still coursing through his veins and he didn't give a flying damn at the moment how she interpreted it.

There was another silence. Lyn's face was pressed into his neck, and after a long moment, he felt a stream of warm air course over him as she exhaled another deep sigh. Her body relaxed then and she melted bonelessly against him in complete and utter trust.

He wanted to tell her he wasn't trustworthy, that with little provocation he could strip her, lift her and turn her so she was straddling his thighs, that her warm, soft curves were giving his body ideas neither one of them was ready for. But she was so vulnerable that he couldn't bring himself to do anything but sit and hold her, praying she wouldn't snuggle any closer and brush her bottom against the hungry flesh stirring at his groin.

They stayed like that for a few minutes longer, but when Tor began to restlessly stamp his feet, Cal used the excuse to lift her from his lap and stood. "I've got to take care of this horse," he told her.

"And I'd better go check on dinner." Lyn didn't look him in the eye as she swiftly walked out of the barn, but in the doorway she paused and looked back. "Thank you."

Her slim body was silhouetted in the light streaming

in the open door and he wondered if she had any idea
how appealing she was, with her quirky curls cascading
over her shoulders and the rise of her breasts defined
clearly. He felt his pulse double and his mouth grew dry.
Before he could answer, she turned away and he was
treated to the sway of her hips as she made her way to
the house.

Damn if she wasn't going to drive him crazy.

A dark, purpling mountain of thunderheads piled up
over the Black Hills several days later. They could see
smoke from several major fires on the Montana prairie,
and he watched the news with a grim expression as the
newscasters detailed the destruction.

They'd butchered a crippled heifer two days earlier and
Lyn had started canning. He wandered into the kitchen
and watched her methodically cutting meat into small
cubes and filling canning jars, then setting them on one
side of the sink to wait for their turn to cook.

"Is there anything I can do?" he asked, feeling guilty.
She'd worked all day and she was still going strong while
he'd been lounging in front of the television.

She shrugged her shoulders, never breaking her
rhythm. "Not really. In a few minutes you could get
those jars off the stove and set new ones in the water."

He nodded, watching the way the muscles in her slender arms flexed as she wielded the knife. "I never knew
how to do this before. Did you learn this from your
mother?"

Her hands stilled on the knife. Slowly, she raised her
head and looked at him, and there was an unreadable
expression on her face. "My mother died when I was
five. I learned to cook and can and clean from my aunt

and the neighbors who were kind enough to let me hang around their kitchens.''

"I'm sorry," he said. "My mother isn't dead but I was raised by my father, too.''

"I know. Silver mentioned it.'' She resumed her methodical cubing. "You could take those jars out now.''

Cal rose and did as she asked. The clock on the wall caught his eye, and a memory made him grin. "Guess what we were doing this time last Friday night?'' he asked her.

She thought for a moment and then the light dawned. A slow smile spread across her face, lighting up her small features until she glowed. "Watching Marty's marriage candidate get pie-eyed.'' She started to laugh, shaking her head ruefully, then added tactfully, "She was beautiful, wasn't she?''

"I don't remember.''

When she glanced at him with startled eyes, he chuckled. "That's the diplomatic response any man who values his life would make.''

She shook the knife at him. "You can't fool me, Cal McCall. If you don't remember what she looked like, it's because you were too busy staring at her other main attributes.''

"What attributes?'' he asked innocently. "The woman was utterly forgettable. I don't remember a thing.''

"Don't you mean 'udderly'?''

He laughed aloud. Then he sobered as he remembered the phone call that had come just before dinner. "The lawyer called today while you were out watering those bushes you planted.''

Her head shot up again. "What did he say?''

Cal sighed. "The sheriff's department wants to talk to

you. He believes it would be in your best interest to go in and talk with them before they issue a subpoena."

"But I can't tell them anything!" Her voice rose in agitation; she set down the knife and wiped her hands on a nearby towel. "They won't believe me when I say I don't remember."

"Yes, they will." He couldn't stand the frightened look that froze her features; he came around the kitchen island to her side and put an arm around her shoulders. "If necessary, we'll get a psychologist to say that you have a memory loss regarding those last weeks in Rapid City. And the medical report of your injuries the day Silver found you will support that." He hesitated, then led her to a chair at the table and pulled her down beside him. "I know you can't remember much, but tell me what you *do* remember."

She shrugged helplessly. "My old boss, a veterinarian in Rapid City, offered me my job back after my divorce. I was living over in Sioux Falls but I didn't like it and I wanted to come home, so I took him up on it." Her hands clenched on the towel. "After I came back to town, my ex-husband came around again and wanted money. I called the police and got a restraining order...and that's all I remember until I woke up in the hospital."

Damn. He could see how this could be a real ugly mess. She very well could have killed the guy, although he knew if she had it had been self-defense, and he wasn't going to stand by and watch her be prosecuted for it. He put a hand over her fingers where they twisted the dish towel repeatedly. "Stop worrying. I told you I'm not going to let anything happen to you."

She stopped twisting the towel and slowly looked up at him. "Why are you being so nice to me?" she whispered.

He tried to ignore the full, pink lips that begged him to lower his head and kiss her. "Because I've gotten used to having a great housekeeper and I don't intend to deprive myself," he said, squeezing her hand lightly before forcing himself to rise and walk away. "I'm going on up to bed now. See you in the morning."

Three

―――

"Cal? Are you in here?" At the sound of Lyn's voice, Cal looked up from the worn bridle he was repairing three days later. Another thing to put on the list of equipment to be replaced. He'd known the ranch would require a hefty cash infusion to restore it to what it had been during his father's lifetime, but it was looking more and more like a bottomless money pit. Good thing his pockets were deep, thanks to his skill at working the market to advantage.

"Cal?"

"Yeah, I'm here."

"The phone's for you."

Setting the bridle aside, Cal rose and walked toward the extension phone on the wall of the barn. "Who is it?" he asked Lyn.

She shook her head. "Sorry. I didn't ask."

"Thanks." He reached for the handset, his gaze on

Lyn's smooth gait as she turned and walked toward the barn door. "McCall."

"Mr. McCall. It's Pat Haney."

Damn. The lawyer he'd engaged calling again so soon probably didn't mean anything good. "What's up, Pat?"

"The Pennington Sheriff's Department definitely wants to talk to Ms. Hamill. She needs to come to the office today at two o'clock. I'll be going with her."

"So will I," said Cal in a grim tone. "I gather this is her only opportunity to come in on her own?"

"Yeah." The attorney sighed. "Apparently they don't have a hope of another lead. Has she remembered anything?"

"No." In the days since they'd discussed the murder, he hadn't brought the subject up because he'd seen how it upset Lyn. "I doubt she ever will," he said somberly. "She had some pretty ugly injuries when Silver found her. The doctors say she may never regain any memories from the time immediately preceding her beating."

Haney sighed again. "Damn. I'm not sure they have enough to charge her on, but I have to be frank with you, they're surely looking hard at her. This could be tricky."

"What do they have?"

"Next to nothing, other than the coroner's estimated time of death, which places it fairly close to Ms. Hamill's hospitalization. And that's the problem. There's no indication that anyone else was involved. This looks like a domestic dispute that turned nasty."

"Lyn wouldn't kill anyone. If she did it, it was accidental. Did you get the copies of the hospital records? You can see what was done to her. Maybe she struck back in self-defense and got lucky."

"The man was shot between the eyes and stuffed in a closet."

"She didn't kill him on purpose," Cal repeated, his voice firming. "If you don't believe that, then I'll have to look for someone else to represent her."

"You might have to, anyway, if they charge her with murder. I'd want someone better versed in defense to step in if that happens." The attorney paused. "I believe you. And I know you believe her. I just hope you're right."

As he hung up the phone and stepped out of the barn, the words rang in Cal's head. *I just hope you're right.* He was. He knew Lyn hadn't murdered anybody as surely as he knew he himself hadn't. Maybe, as he'd said, she'd tried to defend herself and accidentally killed her former husband...but that didn't explain how he'd come to be hidden in a basement. There had to be someone else in the picture.

Three hours later, he sat beside her as two detectives from Rapid City questioned her about her ex-husband. Pat Haney sat on her other side, interrupting occasionally when he felt the detectives' questions stepped over boundaries better established early on.

"Tell us about your relationship with Wayne Galloway," demanded the younger man. His name tag read Det. Amick. Detective Amick had a face like a bulldog and the disposition of a rabid wolf. His hard brown eyes doubted every word Lyn uttered.

Lyn's hand fluttered. "He was my husband. We divorced eighteen months ago."

"Your marriage wasn't a good one, was it?"

"No." She was so pale Cal was worried that she might faint, and her voice was barely audible.

"You filed a restraining order last March. Why?"

Her hands were linked in her lap, clutching each other so tightly her fingertips went white. "Wayne started harassing me after I came back to the area. He came to my apartment several times asking for money. I told him I was barely making it as it was and he got angry. Abusive, like he'd been when we were married. So I called the police and he was warned to stay away.'' She raised haunted eyes to the men across the table. ''Judging from my condition when I woke up in the hospital, I don't guess he did.''

''What happened that day, Ms. Hamill?''

''I don't know.''

''You don't remember.'' Amick uttered the words in a sarcastic tone.

Cal put a hand over Lyn's where they were still clutching each other in her lap. ''If she remembered who beat her, she'd want to tell you, wouldn't she? Why would she hide that?''

''That's what we'd like to know,'' said the older man in a placatory tone. Biddle was the one they'd met at the ranch, and though he wasn't exactly friendly, his partner's attitude made him seem positively cuddly. He sounded like a television cop playing the good-guy role, hoping the poor, off balance subject would confide in him.

''How long have you known Mr. McCall?'' Detective Amick's voice was so brusque Lyn's head came up and a deep red suffused her neck, quickly spreading up her cheeks clear to her hairline. ''I—I, ah…''

''My sister found her after she'd been beaten damn near senseless,'' Cal said. ''I needed a housekeeper and my sister talked me into giving Lyn the job.'' He shot a warning look across the table. ''We met in July when I visited her at the women's shelter. She's been an exemplary employee and I don't appreciate your insinuations.''

''Ms. Hamill is cooperating fully with your investigation,'' Lyn's attorney reminded the men. ''Do you have further questions?''

The detectives looked at each other. The look said that they were convinced Lyn had killed her ex-husband, but equally clearly, they had no proof. ''Not at this time,'' Amick said grudgingly. ''But we might need to talk to you again so don't go anywhere.''

Cal leaned across the table, watching both men steadily. Although neither detective moved, the tension level in the room rose a notch. ''Are you telling Ms. Hamill she is forbidden to travel? On what authority? Can she leave Rapid City? How about Jackson County? Or does she have to stay inside the state borders—''

''We're not restricting her movements,'' said the older detective quickly. He addressed Lyn again. ''We'd just appreciate it if you'd be available should we want to ask other questions.''

''Thank you.'' Pat Haney didn't give either man a chance to comment further. ''If you're finished with Ms. Hamill, we'll go.''

Outside the building, the air was mild and the sun was shining. It was a pleasant day for early October, when the temperature could be anywhere from twenty to sixty. Lyn was shaking visibly as they stood on the street corner waiting for the traffic to pass. Pat had left them to head over to the courthouse and Cal put an arm beneath her elbow as they waited.

''Don't worry,'' he said. ''They can't prove you killed him.''

She pulled away from his hand. ''I *didn't* kill him. I just can't believe I would forget that if I'd done it.''

''All right.'' He kept his tone low and soothing. No sense in getting her stirred up about it. ''Stop worrying. We'll get it straightened out eventually.''

"That was awful." Her voice trembled. "I wish I *could* remember what happened. I'd like to be able to look those men in the eye and tell them I didn't have anything to do with Wayne's death." She shivered even more.

He passed his arm around her waist and tucked her into his side as the light signaled them to cross, matching his longer stride to hers. "Maybe you'll remember what happened one of these days."

"Maybe." Her voice was doubtful. She heaved an immense sigh. "Let's get out of here. I just want to be home."

And so did he. He liked the way the word sounded rolling off her tongue. The easy rhythm of his days on the ranch had come to be defined by Lyn's presence. By the meals she made, the way his clothes smelled after she'd laundered them, by the silence that lay comfortably between them at night as she crocheted while they watched the evening news.

It occurred to him that without her, his home would be just another house, a place for his physical needs. With Lyn around, it was a place to soothe his soul. He'd come to depend on her presence. Not, he assured himself, in a romantic way, but as a part of his life that would leave a void if she weren't there.

Oh, he wasn't above lust. He was definitely interested in the feminine shape that was revealed occasionally beneath her work clothes, and there were times when he was sorely tempted to pursue the attraction that tugged at his senses.

But he wasn't about to pursue anything more than the employer-employee friendship that they currently shared. Lyn was too valuable to him as a friend and employee for him to go screwing it up with sex.

* * *

Someone was chasing her. She'd been hiding and he'd found her! She screamed as she ran frantically through a maze of rooms, each leading into another but none leading to an exit from the menace behind her. She could hear him breathing as he approached, and she knew, with a fatalistic kind of acceptance, that she couldn't run fast enough to escape—

Lyn started upright, the sound of her own whimpering still echoing in the night calm. A trickle of sweat rolled from her temple down her cheek and she absently dabbed at it with the sheet before throwing back the cover and rising. She paced the length of the room several times, collecting herself. After downing most of a cup of water, she marched to the bed and climbed in, pulling the sheet over her and staring at the darkened ceiling.

You just had a bad dream. Relax. Go back to sleep. But she couldn't shake the dream memory of the sick feeling of discovery.

Forty minutes and a lot of clock-watching later, she was still staring at the darned ceiling.

She couldn't get back to sleep because she simply couldn't close her eyes and turn off her brain. Had the detectives believed her this afternoon? She doubted it. Were they going to arrest her? Who had killed Wayne? A thousand things were parading around in her head.

To distract herself from the worries gnawing at her, she let herself think about Cal. His arm around her today had been a sweet moment. Though she was sure he'd only intended it to be a comforting gesture, her stomach had contracted sharply when his long muscular legs had brushed hers and she'd taken a deep breath around the butterflies that invaded her chest when his big hand settled at her waist.

Thinking of Cal led to another thought, the most dangerous one of all, a thought that had nothing to do with her worries for her own liberty. Instead, a very different memory insistently called for her attention.

I just need to get laid. And I'd prefer to do it with somebody I like and enjoy spending time with.

She'd come downstairs for a glass of water that night just in time to hear Cal's deep voice growling out his frustration. Electrified, she'd stood frozen to the floor for a moment, but when the sound of his voice grew louder as he looked toward the door, she'd turned and fled back to her bedroom.

But his rough voice had lingered in her memory ever since.

He'd held her against him a few days ago when she'd been so upset and he'd comforted her—and part of her had wanted to press her lips to his, forgetting about anything besides the hot, thrilling touch of his hands and mouth. And that was when the daring idea had come to her.

Could she offer herself to him?

He'd said he needed…a woman. *She* was a woman.

He'd done so much—given her a place to live, food, the very clothing she wore…but even more important, he'd given her back her self-esteem. If he needed a woman, couldn't she be that woman?

And if she was a woman who wanted him so badly her knees shook when he walked into the kitchen at the end of the day, he'd never have to know. But she wasn't just a woman who wanted him. It wasn't hard to admit it to herself. She loved Cal McCall like she had never loved anyone in her entire life.

She sat upright on the side of the double bed in the room Cal had given her and reached for the water on the table beside the bed. Taking a deep swallow, she considered her courage. Could she do it?

Sex with Wayne had been uninspiring, occasionally painful and always mercifully short. She'd taken steps early in the marriage to prevent a pregnancy when she'd realized what Wayne was like, but she'd stayed with him, like a stupid cow, for three years. Years during which the sex had gotten worse and worse, degenerating into nothing more than another way for Wayne to break her spirit and force her submission. She'd come to loathe it, and with the loathing had come a slow but growing need to fight for herself, both physically and mentally. Her efforts had been futile until she'd woken up one morning with two black eyes and a broken rib and realized she might not live to see thirty if she didn't get away from him.

There had been no sex in her life since her divorce. Not only because she feared it, but because the mere idea repelled her. But it didn't repel her when she thought about making love with Cal. He was the first man who'd gotten underneath her guard and he didn't even know he'd done it.

The fear was another matter. She hadn't been afraid of him since her very first days at the ranch, when the mere shadow of a large man had unnerved her. Cal had simply ignored the way she jumped when he came into a room, the way she'd put a piece of furniture or the counter between them, and eventually she'd forgotten why she'd ever thought she needed to be afraid of Cal. But what would happen if he ever...if she succeeded...

She didn't fear his touch anymore. She'd been held against him and the feeling had been comforting rather than frightening. Well, maybe *comforting* wasn't quite the right word. Her pulse had sped up and her body had felt hot and jittery beneath his big, hard hands. No, comforting wasn't how it felt to be touched by Cal.

A grumble of thunder distracted her from the turmoil in her mind and she drifted over to the window. She wouldn't sleep until the storm passed. Every rancher around dreaded the lightning as much as they welcomed the rain that came with a good storm.

The window was closed since the air-conditioning was working, but she opened it anyway. A hot breath of air fanned over her and she could hear the rustle of leaves in the trees close to the house. Maybe they'd get some rain out of this storm.

A flash of lightning sizzled down from the heavens and she held her breath, counting slowly. Fifteen miles away. The storm was coming from the west and as she stood silently waiting, she could see repeated bolts of white light streak toward the dry ground. Flash...six miles away...flash...three miles away...flash...

And then she saw it.

One terrific bolt of blinding light zigzagged viciously out of the thunderclouds. It struck a hillock maybe two miles away, on land that was either Cal's or Wilson's, and almost immediately she saw the telltale leap of red-gold flame.

"Cal!" she screamed. "Fire!" Her mind cleared of everything but the need to get to work. She grabbed her socks and jeans and stomped into her boots, forgetting a belt. She'd slept in an oversize T-shirt that had belonged to Cal when he was a younger, smaller man and she didn't take the time to grab undergarments but simply stuffed the shirt into her jeans as she bolted into the hallway.

She tore down the stairs and grabbed the phone, called in the fire while Cal charged down the stairs behind her.

He was yanking a T-shirt over his head as he grabbed his hat and the truck keys off the hook beside the door. Seconds after the door banged shut behind him she heard the rev of the pickup's engine. He had a tank full of water by the time she got out the door, and she took a moment to race into the barn and grab a big, dusty bundle of feed sacks before flinging herself into the passenger seat. He blasted the horn as he drove to wake up anyone within earshot.

Cal didn't waste time taking the roads. They bumped across the pastures, with Cal stopping long enough for her to jump out and open the gates and swing them wide for the others who would follow. She braided her hair into a single long plait with frantic fingers and wound it on top of her head, jamming her hat over it. Long, loose hair would be a distinct liability in a fire zone. It was their neighbor Wilson's land, she saw, that had taken the first strike. But she knew that wouldn't matter if the fire got a good start. It would burn everything in its path.

Wilson and his hired men were already beating at the edges of the flames with wet gunnysacks when Cal slammed the truck to a stop near the fire. As they soaked their own bags and began the tiresome, dangerous ordeal, she could see lines of lights coming toward them from both the main road and from the Stryker outfit on Cal's other side. Sirens in the distance heralded the imminent arrival of fire trucks with more volunteers. Cal's hands roared in moments later with more feed bags and water.

Lyn grabbed a sack and soaked it with water, then ran to the nearest point where tongues of fire licked along the ground. More and more trucks roared in and more and more ranch folks joined them. The fire trucks came screaming to a halt and the hoses were unrolled and put to good use, soaking areas of ground far faster than could men on foot. Cal was right on her heels and for a while she was aware of him working off to her left side but eventually her concentration narrowed to a tiny point of focus as she forced back the hungry flames. She beat at the fiery opponent for what seemed like hours, returning to the tank to wet her sack again and again until her muscles burned, until her mind switched off and she worked on automatic pilot, steadily encroaching on the wall of flames that roared and shot into the air. When her feet began to feel hot she looked down to see smoke curling from the soles of her boots, and she quickly soaked them to put out any dangerous embers. A young girl behind her chased down and soaked out flaming cow chips, light enough to be gusted into dry territory by the wind the flames generated, where they lit new fires every place they touched.

It seemed like forever that they fought the flames. Lyn glanced around once, but Cal was gone. As dawn pearled the eastern sky, exhausted firefighters slowed their pace as they won the battle. She walked along the edges of the line, kicking smoldering cow chips back into the burned zone and beating out missed sparks. She was so tired she could barely put one foot in front of the other.

A woman's voice calling her name finally penetrated her daze and she turned, then walked toward a person beckoning with an upflung hand from a truck where people had gathered to scarf down sandwiches sent out from town. The people straggling in were an odd-looking bunch. One rancher still wore striped pajama bottoms, another had forgotten a shirt, though Lyn noted with distant, exhausted amusement that neither man had forgotten his hat. Everywhere she looked, faces were black with smoke and soot.

Silver Stryker greeted her warmly when she drew

close, handing her a sandwich and a steaming cup of cowboy coffee strong enough to put hair on her chest.

"Take a break," Silver told her. "It's under control."

Lyn nodded dully. "Just a short one."

As Silver turned to hand another man something to eat, Lyn wandered off. She glanced at the sandwich and decided she was too tired to eat, so she handed both food and drink to a passing cowboy. Leaning against someone's pickup, she closed her eyes...just for a moment, she promised herself, and then she had to find Cal.

Cal strode wearily toward the food trucks, urgency lengthening his steps. He'd gotten separated from Lyn hours ago and worry nagged at his mind. Sure, she was an experienced ranch woman, but fire was unpredictable and she was still recuperating from her ordeal a few months ago. She worked like a Trojan around the ranch, but he knew she still tired easily; he spent half his time and energy trying to keep her from working too hard and the other half trying to keep her from figuring out that he was protecting her from herself.

He was doing his best to stifle such thoughts when a small form crumpled on the ground beside a pickup caught his eye. He recognized the hair immediately, and fear clutched at his throat as he sprinted to Lyn with a speed he didn't know he still had.

Her hat lay on the ground beside her and her hair had come loose from the braid. Curled up in a little ball right there on the ground, she had both hands beneath her cheek and she was sound asleep.

He squatted beside her. "Lyn." He tried again. "Lynnie. Come on, baby, time to wake up." Reaching out with a blackened hand, he traced the curve of her cheek with one finger.

Her eyes opened. She stared blankly up at him for a moment and he figured if his face was as covered with black as hers was she probably didn't recognize him. "It's me. Cal," he added.

Her eyes lit instantly and before he could react, she'd launched herself off the ground and thrown her arms around his neck. "You're safe!"

Off balance, he fell backward with her sprawled over him. She was as filthy with smoke and soot as he was, but her body was warm and soft and her legs tangled with his felt so damn good that he simply lay there for a moment, enjoying. But when distinct, pleasant stirrings of arousal woke within him despite his exhaustion he fell back on flippancy to cover the moment. "Well, hey. How come you don't greet me like this at home?"

She tried to laugh, but a rusty wheeze was all that came out and she immediately started to cough. Alarmed, he rolled over and rose.

"You overdid it," he said accusingly as he scooped her into his arms. She felt so light and frail in his arms that he had to grit his teeth and clamp his jaw closed to keep from yelling at her. What in hell had she been thinking of?

"I did not." But her voice was as hoarse as his from swallowing too much smoke, and she lay against him like a rag doll. "Everybody worked as hard. We got the fire stopped, didn't we?"

"We did." Her voice was surprisingly argumentative, and his anger faded as he smiled to himself over her head. He barely kept himself from commenting that "everybody" hadn't been beaten within an inch of their life a few months ago, but decided that would accomplish nothing. Gently, he opened the door of his pickup and set her on the seat.

As he drew back to examine her face, she exclaimed in dismay. "You're burned!"

He could feel the skin stinging across his cheekbones and wondered if hers felt the same, because it looked as raw and angry as his felt. "Stay here," he ordered.

A couple of the wives had come from town with sandwich fixings and ointment for burns. He grabbed food, bottles of water and some of the medical supplies and headed back to the truck. "Let me put some of this on you," he said as he approached.

Lyn was still sitting where he'd left her, slumped sideways against the back of the seat, but she straightened. "No, you need it worse."

He held the tube out of her reach, though, and pushed her back with a hand on her shoulder when she would have gotten down from the truck. Beneath his big hand, her flesh felt soft over the slender bones of her neck and shoulder, and he pulled his hand away before he gave in to the temptation to slide it over the curve of her breast.

"Nope. Either you sit still and let me put this on you or I'll hold you down and do it," he threatened.

Her eyes flashed green sparks, a funny sight through the soot that darkened her face, then she sat back with quiet dignity. "I don't know why you're bothering," she said in a huffy tone. "What's one more scar on this face?"

Cal froze for a second. She was looking at the ground, and when he put his hand against the side of her face, her head jerked up and her eyes met his. He traced the long line of the fading scar that sliced from her jaw into her lower lip with a featherlight touch. "This is barely noticeable," he told her, forcing her to hold his gaze. "You're going to be as gorgeous as you were before."

Her pupils flared. "I'm not—I was never—"

"You're gorgeous," he said flatly, in no mood for more argument from her. "Now keep quiet and let me put this on your face."

Something in the ferocious tone of his voice must have gotten through to her. She gauged his set expression for one more long moment, then sighed and tilted her face to the sky.

When he'd finished applying the ointment, she took the tube from him and returned the favor. As her delicate hands stroked lightly over his face, soothing the sting from the burns, she let out a quiet sigh. "I was scared to death when I couldn't find you," she said softly, resting one small palm against his cheek.

Her words streaked through him like the lightning from the storm, slowly burning away all rational thought. Her face was close and he stared into her wide green eyes for a long moment until they fluttered closed, his hand coming up to cover hers where it rested on his face. "You gave me a scare, too." To hell with all the appropriate employer-employee relationships he'd been worrying about. Slipping his free arm around her, he pulled her against his body, bringing his lips to rest against her forehead.

Although a part of him leaped to life at the feel of soft feminine flesh, he ignored it. Lyn needed sweetness and comfort. Friendship. Family. She needed to be able to give someone a simple hug without it being misconstrued. That was all this was.

Wasn't it? She didn't stiffen or draw away, merely sighed and let herself flow against him until he could feel every long, slim inch of her from neck to knee. Her body was softly angled, and the firm mounds of her breasts pushed at him, testing his resolve. Grimly, he hung onto control, hoping she didn't feel his rising arousal.

After a moment of silence, punctuated by the weary shuffle of other firefighters heading for their vehicles, she said, "Let's go home." Warm puffs of breath feathered over his throat as she spoke, and a shiver of pure, sexual need clawed its way up his spine.

He loosened his arm and stepped back a pace. "Good idea. You need rest."

At the house, they climbed wearily from the truck and made their way inside. She was weaving on her feet, and he knew she had to be dead tired. He almost reached out to support her but at the last minute drew back his hands. He didn't trust himself.

In the kitchen, she went straight to the cupboards and got down two large glasses, then filled them from the ice and water dispenser on the refrigerator door. She offered him the first one and he took it with a grateful word of thanks, draining the whole thing in moments and getting more for himself while she sipped at hers.

He cleared his throat. "I knew we wouldn't get away without some fire this year. It's been too dry."

"Still, it could have been worse," she said.

"A lot worse." Standing here making small talk was stupid; they both needed sleep. Still, he was reluctant to let her go entirely. "What woke you? You must have seen it almost right away because your hollering woke me and we got over there pretty darn fast."

She shrugged. "I was already awake. Thinking."

"Thinking about what?"

She set her glass on the table, looking away from him. "I had a nightmare and I couldn't get back to sleep. And then my mind started to wander, and I—" Her gaze found his and her eyes were direct and serious. "I was thinking about sex."

He was so shocked and startled he choked on the water

and had to cough to clear his throat. Images of hot, sweaty bodies rolling across white sheets flashed through his head. "Sex?"

She nodded. "And my marriage. A whole lot of ugly things I really, really hope I'll forget someday."

Her voice sounded so hopeless that something inside his chest tightened into a small, aching ball. And it bothered the hell out of him that to her, sex was something *ugly*. She wasn't going to think like that if he had anything to do with it. "Your life is completely different now than it was when you were married," he said forcefully. "*You're* different. And even if you never forget, I'm betting that you won't let it affect the future."

She studied him for a long moment as if he'd spoken in a dialect she didn't quite comprehend. Finally she sighed and sent him the smallest beginning of a smile. "I hope you're right about that."

Four

The first snow fell the following weekend.

Typical South Dakota weather, Lyn thought as she struggled into an old fleece-lined jacket and jammed her hat on her head. When she woke at dawn, the world had been a white wonderland, but just hours later it had warmed up to a balmy sixty degrees and already the snow was half melted and making a slick mess of the lane. The only good thing about it was that it brought welcome moisture to reduce the chance of more fires.

Rushing out the back door, she quickly fed the barn cats and the two dogs that had been at the ranch since Cal had arrived, giving the older dog the anti-inflammatories that kept his arthritis at bay. She'd also taken on the task of nursing sick and injured cattle that Cal had confined in corrals near the house, and she was anxious to get a look at the calf without one hoof she'd been coaxing along.

The poor little fellow had been a difficult birth from an older cow who'd died shortly after. In the struggle to get the calf out alive, the man who'd found her had been tugging to free him, and one of the fragile hooves had slipped right off his foreleg. Cal had assigned one of the men the task of feeding the orphan, but when Lyn arrived, the calf looked like it would expire any day. It had been her first project other than housework, and the calf's survival had come to symbolize her ability to survive, as well.

Now the little fella came hobbling across the pasture toward her, lurching and slipping in the gumbo that the melting snow and clay combined to create. She watched his slow progress, laughing as he walked up and butted her. She didn't fool herself that his attentions had anything to do with affection. "You're a mooch," she told him. "The only time you're sweet to me is when you know it's feeding time."

"Don't get too attached to him." Cal's deep voice came from behind her, and she jumped as if she'd been caught stealing cattle.

"I won't," she said. "I grew up on a ranch, remember? I haven't named him."

Cal only grunted. He walked to the fence and took a position beside her, resting his forearms on the top rail, and she noticed he was dressed nicely, as if he was going to town. "I didn't think he'd make it," he admitted. "You've done a good job with him."

Warmth stole through her. "Thank you."

Cal cleared his throat. "I have to go away for a few days."

"You do?" She was dismayed by the anxiety his words provoked. She was a grown woman who could take care of herself. It was ridiculous to feel this sense of…neediness. It was stupid.

"I have to go to New York." He turned slightly toward her. "I'll only be gone three or four days."

She forced herself to act casual. "I won't plan any six-course meals for the next few days, then."

He chuckled. "Good." Then he did something incredible. *He took her hand.* She shot a glance at his face but he was looking at their joined hands as he slid his much larger fingers through hers where they rested on the fence rail. "Will you be all right here alone?"

"I've been alone before." Her voice sounded strained and breathless, as if she'd run for miles, and she swallowed. He'd held her and kissed her forehead after the fire and she'd nearly made a fool of herself, practically falling into his arms. Was this just another absent gesture or…? She couldn't allow herself to finish the thought.

"When I get back," he said, "I'd like to have a party. Sort of payback for all the kindnesses folks have shown us since I moved back and you came. What do you think?"

She shrugged. "It's your home. If you want to have a party, I'll prepare for a party."

He turned toward her, and she felt his gaze on her. "It's your home, too, now," he said quietly. "If the thought of a large crowd of people bothers you, I won't do it. Deck and Silver would have it at their place if I asked."

She looked up. Mistake. His eyes were a warm blue-gray, framed by thick dark lashes that shouldn't have been wasted on a man. Looking into them gave her a jumpy feeling in the pit of her stomach and made her knees feel trembly. "A party won't bother me," she said. "The women at the shelter had a birthday party for me when I was staying there. I actually enjoyed it.'' She tried to smile, though her lips felt stiff and uncooperative. ''But I appreciate the thought.''

Cal's gaze slid to her mouth. ''All right.'' He continued looking at her mouth as he spoke, and she wondered if he was inspecting the scar that curled into her lip. ''Why don't we say Saturday…around five. There's a list of names on my desk.''

She nodded. He was *still* looking at her mouth, and she licked her lips, running her tongue over the edge of her scar as her nerves began to jitter.

He straightened away from the rail, and his gaze narrowed as he released her fingers. ''I have to leave now.''

Don't go. ''All right.'' She hesitated, then grabbed her courage in both hands and stretched on her tiptoes, touching her lips to the firm line of his in a fleeting kiss. ''Have a safe trip.''

She started to move away but two big hands caught her by the waist. ''Lyn.''

''What?'' She couldn't look at him again; she was sure he was displeased with her familiarity.

''You can do better than that.''

Shock brought her head up. An odd smile was playing around his mouth. She could hardly believe it, but unless she was totally off the mark, he wanted her to kiss him again! Slowly, she came up on tiptoe, bracing her hands on his broad chest. His eyes closed as she brushed her lips over his, and she closed hers, as well. His mouth was surprisingly soft. Then, before she could withdraw, his hands tightened at her waist, holding her in place. His mouth took over the kiss, following hers as he tilted his head slightly to more fully explore the connection.

Shivers of delight rushed from her lips down to her breasts and beyond. She'd dreamed of Cal's kisses for weeks, futile dreams that she'd never expected would come to pass. Moving closer, she made a sound of purring approval deep in her throat.

Cal stilled against her. Slowly, he dragged his lips away, along the angle of her jaw to the hollow just beneath her ear. She felt a single hot flick of his tongue against the tender tissue, then he was drawing back and she opened her eyes rather dazedly to find him smiling at her with that same inscrutable expression.

"Think of me." It was an order, accompanied by the touch of his index finger to her nose before he turned away and strode toward the truck at the edge of the yard.

Think of him? Ha! As if she were likely to do anything else.

She wandered inside, touching her fingers to her lips where she could still feel the pressure of his mouth against hers. What was happening here? She'd never turn Cal away—did he know that?

The telephone rang, cutting short her confused musings. She reached for the handset. "McCall's."

"Hi, Lyn. It's Silver."

"Hello!" Her pleasure at hearing her friend's voice echoed in her response. "How are you feeling?"

Silver chuckled. "Better now that the first trimester's over. Everyone says I'd better enjoy this part of the pregnancy while I can still see my feet."

"You don't have anything to worry about. You've only gained a few pounds so far, right?"

"Yes, but that could change rapidly. Listen, I have some big news for Cal. Can he come to the phone?"

Lyn grimaced, though Cal's half sister couldn't see her. "You just missed him. Business trip. He'll be gone for a few days."

"Oh. Well, I guess it isn't that big a deal. If he calls,

you can tell him Mom's coming to stay for a few days. She'll be arriving on Friday.''

"Your mother's coming to town? That *is* news, isn't it?'' Lyn knew from things Silver had said that her mother had never been back to South Dakota since she'd left when Cal was a baby.

"Yes.'' Silver's voice was fond. "She's planning to come and stay for a few weeks when the baby comes. Deck talked her into coming out for a short trip now, as well. He says we'll be too busy to visit after Deck, Jr. arrives.'' Silver chuckled but then her tone changed. "I hope this will go all right. Mom's really looking forward to seeing Cal but I'm not sure he'll be as pleased.''

"They don't get along?''

"That's not exactly it.'' Silver hesitated. "I think Cal still resents her for leaving him behind when she left. Even when he came to live with us, there was this…wall around him that no one was allowed to get past.''

"Has she ever explained why she left him with your father?''

"Not to me.'' The other woman sounded troubled now. "I always assumed that she thought he'd be better off growing up with a man's influence. When she left, of course, she had no idea she'd remarry.''

Lyn felt odd, discussing things of such a personal nature behind Cal's back. "I'm sure he'll be glad to see her.''

"I hope so.'' Silver sounded dubious. Changing the subject, she inquired about their cattle. From there the talk moved to Lyn's preparations for her first winter back on a ranch. It would be Silver's first ever, and she was somewhat apprehensive about severe weather considering that the baby was due in February.

"I hope you know how to deliver a baby,'' she joked.

Lyn grinned at the apprehension in her friend's voice. "Well, I've helped deliver plenty of four-legged things; I imagine if I had to, I could help deliver a two-legged one. But it won't come to that," she said in the most reassuring tone she could muster. "When you get near your due date, we'll keep a close eye on the weather and the doctor's predictions. If it looks chancy, you can stay at the women's shelter in Rapid where I lived for a while. I already asked Rilla and she said no problem."

There was a silence from the other end of the phone. "Thank you," said Silver in a subdued voice. "And thank Rilla. The day you came to my door was a lucky one for me."

"And for me," Lyn responded, feeling tears sting the backs of her eyelids. She had never had a close female friend in her whole life. Her father had kept her too isolated and she'd missed too much school to ever fit in well and develop the friendships that most of the kids did. And after her marriage, there'd been even less opportunity for feminine companionship.

After a few more warm exchanges, Lyn said goodbye and replaced the phone on its base. How much her life had changed since—

—*she had to hide! Hide before Wayne could find her and hit her again. Her breath sobbed in and out of her lungs as she wedged herself behind the vacuum cleaner and a pile of cleaning supplies in the hall closet. Then— footsteps in the hall just outside the door of the apartment. Sharp rap-rap-rap on the door. Strange man's voice. "Open this door, Galloway. I know you're in there with the little woman. It's time to pay up—"*

And that fast, the moment was gone. Lyn was perched on a stool at the bar where she'd been talking on the phone, and it was a good thing, because she suspected she'd have slid to the floor otherwise.

Dear God! Had she remembered a *real* occurrence? Or had that been some figment of her imagination wishing for an easy answer? Had there been a third person in her apartment in those hours she couldn't account for between the time she last remembered and the time Silver had found her? Who could it have been? She concentrated, dredging up the memory fragment and replaying the voice. There *was* something vaguely familiar about it…or was she grasping at straws?

Her hands were shaking and she clasped them tightly together on the bar, realizing she was gulping air. Cal. She had to tell Cal—

She was halfway out the door before she realized he wasn't there. And as she stood there, arrested her in flight, she decided that this was the last time she was going to let herself go running to a man to solve her problems. *Why* had she felt it imperative to tell Cal about this? Sure, he'd probably be interested. But she knew in her heart that he'd have taken over the burden of deciding what to do about it. And that she'd have been happy to let him do so. To lean on his strength and rely on him to carry her along.

And that was something she needed to stop. Much as she might wish otherwise, Cal wasn't going to be in her life forever. And in any case, she wanted—needed—to be able to make her own decisions and choices. To rely on her own strength.

Chewing on her lip, she thought about her options. Telling Cal was out. Both because he was away and because it wasn't his problem. Call the sheriff and tell him what she'd remembered? The expressions on the faces of the two detectives stopped that idea cold. They hadn't believed her to start with; they'd be even less likely to believe a half memory. They'd say, and logically so, that she was fabricating a story that wouldn't implicate her.

Really, there was no sense in sharing this with anybody unless she remembered something concrete that would help the investigation.

Cal was going to miss his own party.

Lyn set out the basket of kaiser rolls for the barbecued beef as Deck's truck rolled into the yard. Cal had called on Thursday to say he'd be delayed until Saturday. The news had so disappointed her that she'd completely forgotten to tell him his mother was coming to town.

And now the guests were due to arrive any minute and he still wasn't home. She walked outside, waving as she drew close to the truck. "Hello. I feel a little foolish playing hostess, but Cal isn't back yet."

Deck Stryker grinned, stopping to buss her on the cheek as he strode around to open the other door. "We don't need him to make a party, anyhow."

Silver slid out, laughing at her husband as Deck put a hand firmly under her elbow. "Deck, stop hovering. Being pregnant doesn't mean I can't walk unaided."

An older woman behind her spoke as Deck stepped forward to help her down, as well. "Let him fuss, honey. If he's anything like your daddy, once that baby arrives he'll be so thrilled he'll barely remember your name."

Silver smiled, tucking an arm through her mother's and drawing her forward. "Mama, this is my friend Lyn. She's Cal's housekeeper and the one who generally keeps things running smoothly around here. Lyn, this is my mother, Cora Lee Jenssen."

Lyn looked into gray eyes the exact same shade as Cal's as his mother took her hand in a warm clasp. "It's nice to meet you, Mrs. Jenssen. Welcome to—'' She stopped as she remembered that this woman once had lived here, albeit for a brief time.

"Thank you, honey, and call me Cora Lee, please." She patted Lyn's hand with her free one before releasing her and looking beyond her to the house. "My, my, it certainly looks better than it did when I came here more than thirty years ago." Cora Lee had a slow, distinctly Southern drawl that fell easily on the ear. Strange that Silver didn't have nearly such a thick accent.

"Lyn has a way with growing things," Silver told her mother, indicating the flowers blooming around the door. "She just walks by and smiles and everything blooms."

"That's not true." Lyn gestured to the walkway that led to the house. "Would you like to see the inside? Cal recently finished putting on an addition. Silver oversaw most of the rest of the redecorating and I'm afraid it's painfully obvious where she left off and I carried on."

"Hey, what time's everybody coming?" Deck glanced at his watch.

"We have about twenty minutes," Lyn reminded him.

"I'll keep an eye on the barbecue while you ladies do the house tour," he offered.

Silver snorted. "Got out of that one pretty neatly, didn't you?"

He smiled smugly as he headed for the keg underneath the cottonwood tree beside the house. "A man has to do what a man has to do."

Just then the sound of a truck on the gravel lane reached their ears, and a moment later, it came around the little ridge and down toward the house.

"That's Cal!" Lyn took three hurried steps toward the yard and then stopped abruptly. "He'll be delighted to see you," she said to Cora Lee Jenssen, trying to gloss over her enthusiastic reaction to her boss's return.

Silver laughed softly behind her. "Why don't you go ahead and tell him she's here?"

As Cal pulled his truck into the yard, he thought again of the soft sweetness of Lyn's lips and the warm pressure of her body as she'd let him extend the brief caress. Hell, he'd barely thought of anything else the whole time he'd been gone. What had possessed him to kiss her the day he left? He didn't regret it, but it surely was going to complicate the easy relationship he'd worked so hard to develop with her.

He saw a small knot of people in the yard and recognized his sister, but then Lyn's slim figure detached itself from the group and walked toward him and he forgot about the others. Her hair was caught back in a scarf behind her neck, but a red halo surrounded her head and gleaming strands clung to the shoulders of her denim jacket.

"Hey there," he said, not bothering to conceal the pleasure he felt at the sight of her. Later, he'd analyze just why it felt so good to have her there to greet him, but right now he was going to enjoy.

"Welcome home." Her eyes were bright and warm, and he wondered if she'd missed him. Had she thought about the kiss they'd shared as much as he had?

His fingers itched to reach for her, and before he could remind himself of all the reasons not to, he settled his hands at her waist and drew her close. "I hated being away."

She placed her palms against the front of his leather coat. "I...didn't like you being away." Her voice was the same throaty, husky murmur that haunted his dreams and left him aching and unfulfilled in the mornings. Though he knew it was due to injury, he found himself hoping she wouldn't lose the incredibly sexy tones.

She cleared her throat and he realized he was staring at her mouth. It was hard not to. Her lips were full and perfectly bowed, and every movement of her mouth when she spoke was a sensual feast.

"We have a special guest today."

"Oh?" He couldn't care less. He was sorry that he'd decided on this party; all he wanted to do was explore the growing awareness between them. Ah, who was he kidding? What he really wanted was to strip her naked and lay her flat on her back in his big bed for about six weeks straight.

"Your mother's in town for a few days."

"That's great—*what?*" He shook his head, sure he hadn't heard her clearly.

"Your mother came out to stay with Silver for a few days. She's standing right back there."

"You're joking." Every ounce of pleasure he'd felt at the homecoming vanished as he lifted his head and saw a petite blonde standing beside Silver. His mother. Fury rushed through him. "Did you know about this?" he demanded.

She stepped out of reach and he realized his grip on her waist had tightened to the point where he'd probably hurt her. Her eyes were huge green pools of confusion. "Yes. I meant to tell you when you called but I forgot—"

"Never mind." He cut off the explanation with a short, sharp gesture.

"Cal? What's wrong?" She followed him as he stepped around her and moved toward his family.

What's wrong? Oh, nothing, except that my mother

abandoned me without a backward glance thirty years ago. He stopped in front of his sister and his mother, pulling out the manners with which he was determined his genteel Southern mama would never find fault. "Well, what a surprise. Welcome back to South Dakota, Mother." He took the hands she extended before she could hug him and skimmed a fleeting kiss over her still-smooth cheek.

"And sister dear." His voice warmed with genuine affection as he stepped in to kiss Silver, hugging her close for a brief instant. "Still glowing, I see. Everything going well?"

"Everything's going fine." Silver was eyeing him with a frown but she resisted blurting out the questions he could see in her accusing gaze. "Mama's going to come and stay when the baby's born so she decided to get a jump on remembering the lifestyle out here."

The lifestyle that didn't suit her well enough to stay and raise her child.

He nodded, not wanting to get into a discussion of anything involving his mother. Then, to his relief, a car came around the ridge, followed by two trucks. The party was beginning, and he could ignore this problem until it went away. Excusing himself, he went back to the truck and grabbed his bag, then headed for a quick shower and clean clothes.

Even though the chilly air grew significantly cooler after the sun went down, the party was a rousing success. Judging from the late hour at which the last of his guests departed, Cal could honestly say they'd had a heck of a good time.

Too bad he couldn't say the same about himself. He doused the grill with water for the last time and checked to be sure there was nothing left on the long folding table

Lyn had set out, but the women had cleaned up everything. Even the table cover was gone.

He stepped through the mudroom into the kitchen, hanging his hat and jacket on their hooks. Glancing at his watch, he decided it was too late to watch the weather. He'd catch it tomorrow. One of the other ranchers had said it was supposed to get cold over the weekend.

As he put up a hand to switch off the kitchen lights, Lyn walked in from the living room with her hands full of used paper cups and plates. "Wait right there," she said. "I have to toss these out. I forgot to check the inside of the house when we were cleaning up."

He waited, one hand on the light switch. As she dumped the load into the trash, she glanced at him. "I didn't mean it literally."

He should have grinned and said something light. Instead, he said, "I'm sorry if I gave you the impression I was angry with you earlier."

Her head came up, and she held his gaze as she moved to the sink to wash her hands. "Apology accepted." Pause. "Who *were* you angry with, then?"

He shrugged. "Nobody. Seeing my mother here just caught me off guard."

"You weren't pleased to see her."

He exhaled heavily, and his hand fell away from the switch. "It was a surprise."

Lyn was silent. She dried her hands on a dish towel and slowly, methodically folded it over the oven handle.

"I grew up out here with my father," he found himself saying. "I don't know her that well."

One dark eyebrow rose, then her expressive face settled into a smooth blank mask. "The only memory I have of my mother is this song she used to sing at bedtime.

She sat on the edge of my bed and rubbed my back and sang.''

"I don't have any memories of my mother from my childhood," he said, not even knowing why he was telling her. "She left my father and me and went back to Virginia before I was a year old. I never even met her until I was six and my father sent me to visit for a week one summer. After that, I went every summer. For a week or two. Then after I graduated high school I lived there for a little while until I started college."

Lyn knew why he'd left Kadoka after high school. Deck Stryker's twin sister had died in that accident, and Deck had blamed Cal at the time. "Have you ever asked her why she left?"

"I know why. It was too rough and rural for her. Not as *civilized* as good ol' Virginny."

"But have you ever talked to her about it?"

"No." He reached up abruptly and switched off the lights. "I'm bushed. Good night."

"You should, you know." Her voice came from behind him in the darkened kitchen. "While you still can."

He stepped aside and allowed her to precede him out of the kitchen. She was a silent shadow in the nighttime quiet of the old house, but he could discern the straight line of her back as she walked ahead of him toward the stairs. As she set one foot on the first step, he reached out and caught her wrist. Instantly, she stilled, but she didn't turn to face him.

"Don't judge me," he said in a low voice.

She did turn then, stepping back down. Her hair drifted around her and he could smell the clean scent of the fragrance his sister had given her for her birthday. And though it had to be his imagination, he could feel the heat of her body only inches from his, searing him with hot interest.

"I'm not judging you." Her voice was low, too, aimed at the floor.

"You're not happy with me." Her wrist felt so fragile beneath his big hand that he was sure one careless move could break a bone. Slowly, stealthily, he stroked his thumb along the delicate veins he could feel beneath the skin. Her pulse beat there and he pressed lightly, counting the rapid beats in silence.

"No," she said, still looking down. "I'm not. I'm saddened. Disappointed. You're a good person, Cal. You took me in out of the kindness of your heart. I can't believe you wouldn't extend that same kindness to your own mother."

The words stung. He seized on the one statement that he could face. "I told you when you came that I'd give you a chance and you could stay if you could handle it. You've earned a place here. I'm not motivated by kindness."

He lifted his other hand and circled her neck, using his thumb beneath her chin to lift her head. Her eyes gleamed in the shadowed night; then she lowered her lids. He inspected her features and his thumb crept up to probe at her bottom lip.

"Why did you kiss me the other day?" He could tell by the way her eyes snapped wide and her body jerked a little bit that he'd startled her with the change of topic.

The silence stretched breathlessly as their eyes caught, held, spoke of things unsaid. Then she shrugged, a small smile curving the corners of her lovely lips. "It seemed like the thing to do."

He nodded, considered. "How does it feel now?"

"Like…" She smiled, a shy smile that held growing

knowledge, and her eyes caught the moonlight and sparkled. "Like the thing to do?"

She was tired; so was he. It probably was a huge mistake, but he was sick of forcing himself to back away from the woman every cell in his body told him to touch. With intense deliberation, he slid one arm around her, his gaze locked with hers. Then control fell away and he swiftly pulled her against him, forcing her legs to part and pressing himself into her body. He heard her draw in a startled breath. His other hand shifted to clasp her chin and he placed his mouth on hers, swamped by an overwhelming sense of relief at the feel of her soft mouth beneath his.

She was as still as a doe in a meadow beneath his hands. Losing himself in the experience, he molded her lips for long moments, barely aware that she was beginning to respond as his body urged him on. This was the woman he wanted, the woman he'd dreamed of every day for weeks. Using his tongue to trace the outline of her lips, he flicked it lightly across the closed seam until her body relaxed in his arms. She made a soft sound, a sigh or moan, deep in her throat, and a hot rush of awareness coursed through him. She was pliant and willing, exactly as he'd wanted her to be, and she was *real*.

Her palms slipped into his hair, spearing through it to cradle his scalp. It felt so intimate that he shifted again, moving both hands to her back to stroke and mold her to his longer, larger frame. He slanted his head and deepened the kiss, using his tongue to open her lips, slipping inside and then sucking her tongue lightly, encouraging her to explore his mouth as he explored hers. When her tongue tentatively met his, he groaned deep in his throat and a shudder worked its way down his backbone. Her delicate hands slipped down to grip his shoulders, and he dragged a hand to the back of her neck, plunging it deep into the thick mass of her hair and holding her head still.

His body was on fire, burning as hot as the prairie grass had last week, and he tightened his arm around her waist, drawing her onto her toes. He walked her backward until she came up against the wall, until all that held her up was his hard, aching body pinning her in place. His breath caught in his throat; he thrust his hips against her again and again in a mindless haze of need. His body had been begging for her touch for days and it felt better, more right than anything ever had before in his life. Within minutes, he could feel the urgent beat of impending release rushing through him with relentless force. He had to have her *now*. Putting a hand between them, he fumbled for the zipper on her jeans—

And then someone whimpered. A hand came down and closed over his, breaking his concentration, and he realized it was Lyn whimpering, Lyn's hand clasped tightly about his.

He froze. So did Lyn, her slim body growing stiff and still in his embrace.

Holy hell! He released her as if she were boiling and stepped back as her feet touched the ground, spinning to face away from her. Scrubbing both hands over his face, he took a long moment to remember who and where he was as he forced himself to ignore the raging demands of his flesh. What had happened?

What do you mean, what happened? The inner voice was mocking. *You almost took your own employee by force.*

"Lyn—" His voice was deep and strained. "My God, Lyn, I'm sorry. I don't know what I was thinking—" Well, that wasn't true, but... "There's no excuse for my behavior. I promise you it will never happen again."

Is that a promise you're going to be able to keep?

Of course it was. He wasn't an animal, driven by instinct. He was a man. And Lyn was a woman who'd been manhandled enough in her life. Remorse struck and he flinched beneath its whip as he remembered the hell of a marriage she'd been trapped in. What had his thoughtless mauling done to her?

There was silence behind him, and he realized she still hadn't said a word. In fact, he didn't think she'd moved at all. His mind flashed a vivid mental picture of her cowering against the wall as he slowly turned around. And his worst fears were realized.

She *hadn't* moved. One hand covered the luscious lips he'd been devouring. Another memory intruded and he forced himself to forget that for a moment or two, *or more,* her mouth had moved under his and her tongue had joined his in a seeking, slippery dance of foreplay.

He swore violently under his breath, and her eyelids flinched, as if each word were a stroke of a whip on her soft skin. "Lyn," he said again. "I'm sorry. If you want to leave, I'll understand. I'm sure you can stay with Silver. I can take you over there right now and have someone bring your things tomorrow—"

She dropped her hand from her mouth, and her eyes flared wide in the shadows. "Are you dismissing me?"

"Of course not." He was making a huge hash of this.

"I'd like to keep my job." Her voice was low and intense, huskier than usual, and his damned stupid body reacted to the throaty, sexy tone as if it hadn't figured out the fun was over.

"I'd like you to keep your job," he said. "I swear you'll never have to worry about me manhandling you again."

Her eyes grew blank and she dropped her gaze from

his. After another tense moment of silence, she turned from him and walked sedately up the stairs, treating him to an eyeful of rounded bottom that did nothing to quell the fires inside him.

His body was still hard and throbbing, but he was so glad she hadn't run screaming that he didn't say a word. He started to the second floor behind her, castigating himself with every step. What was wrong with him, forcing himself on a defenseless soul like Lyn? Granted, he wanted her with an almost painful intensity every day, but he knew that was only a reaction to their forced proximity. He just needed to get away from her for a little while, maybe call that widow in Rapid or meet some other woman with whom he could have a hot, harmless fling, and then everything would be fine.

If that's all you need, then why didn't you jump Marty's date the other week?

Shut up, he wanted to snarl at the voice in his head. He reached the top of the stairs and tried one more time, aiming his words at the back of her head.

"Lyn, I'm sorry. I'll say it as many—"

"Don't apologize." Her voice carried a snap of authority that surprised him and shut him up in midsentence. Then she whirled, and the look in her eyes froze him in his tracks. She placed a hand right in the middle of his chest, palm flat against him, searing his flesh like a hot branding iron. "In three years of marriage, my husband's kisses never made me feel like that. I'm not sorry and I'd rather you weren't, either."

As her words rang in his head, he turned them over and over. He'd frightened her. Hadn't he? He'd practically forced her. Hadn't he? He wasn't sure of anything at the moment except that somehow, someway, Lyn had forgiven him already for his crude advance.

No. She hadn't just forgiven him, he realized. She'd *liked* his touch, his caress, his kiss. As he struggled to fit together the confusing pieces of the puzzle that was his housekeeper, the heated emerald of desire that had shone from her eyes lingered in his mind, prodding his body with inescapable memories, making it impossible to forget how she'd felt wrapped around him earlier. And as she said good-night and disappeared into her room at the other end of the hall from his, he wondered where in hell this crazy attraction was going.

He couldn't see an end, couldn't imagine one that wasn't messy and hurtful. And that made him pause. He *liked* Lyn. Both as a friend and as a hardworking faithful employee. And he knew that as badly as he wanted her, sex would ruin all that. He might be on fire for her now, but he'd been on fire for women before and had managed to resist leaping into the flames.

He'd just have to resist this time, too.

Five

An inch of ice had formed on the stock tanks and over the dam when Cal checked the next day. It was a sure sign the weather was turning. He broke the ice and then started distributing cake since the grass was too short to fatten the cattle.

He got into the yard in midafternoon with three cows and calves that needed to be weaned. The bawling was still echoing in his head when he went into the house to clean up and start on the monthly ledger.

Lyn was in the kitchen rolling out something with a rolling pin and he hollered hello, then went to take a shower. She was still working at it when he came into the kitchen twenty minutes later.

Strolling over to the counter, he eyed her work. "Pie dough?" he asked hopefully, letting her know from his tone that he was willing to keep it light if she was. He wondered how things would be between them after last night.

She shook her head. "Slippery pot pie. I had a taste for it." She smiled at him and he saw that her eyes were faraway in another time. "My aunt used to make it."

"Your aunt?" Lyn rarely spoke of herself or her childhood and he was curious. Just natural, he told himself. *I'd be curious about anyone.*

"After my mother died, she used to take me over to her place every now and then. I wouldn't know beans about cooking if it wasn't for her."

"Judging from your skills, she must have known more than beans," he said honestly. "You're a great cook."

"Thanks." Her fair skin flushed lightly beneath the golden freckles that dotted her face.

"You've never mentioned any family. If you'd like to invite anyone over, it's not a problem."

Her face closed up instantly. "My aunt isn't living anymore. She was the only family I had other than my father."

Her hands were clenched into small fists over the handles of the rolling pin and he reached across the counter and laid his palms over hers, gently prying her fingers off the handles and straightening them out of their tense state. "I didn't mean to make you think of unhappy things." And it was true. It was just that he was intensely curious about Lyn's childhood. She'd told him little more than he already knew, that she'd grown up without a mother on an isolated ranch with an alcoholic father. How had she stayed so sweet, so soft and gentle? Why hadn't she grown tough, lost the air of innocence that surrounded her like the subtle perfume she wore when she dressed up?

"It's all right." She exhaled slowly, then picked up

the roller again. "My memories of my aunt are wonderful ones. She was warm and funny and she used to bake chocolate-chip cookies every time I came over."

"Mrs. Stryker used to make cookies a lot." It was one of his own fond memories. "I never had anything like that around since it was just me and Dad, and going over there was like heaven." He smiled. "I should have learned to bake them."

"You should have." She grinned at him. "Who says a man can't learn to cook?"

"I can cook now," he informed her with great dignity. "In New York, I lived alone in an apartment. It was either cook or eat takeout for every meal."

"What's it like? In New York, I mean?" Her tone was unconsciously longing.

"Rushed. Like an anthill. People hurrying everywhere you look." He chuckled. "It's impossible to imagine unless you see it for yourself. The buildings are so high you feel like you can't get enough air or light. It's exciting. But I never got used to it."

"But you were there for..."

"Six years. And I never stopped looking out my window expecting to see prairie. When I decided to move back, I felt like I'd finally taken the step I'd been considering for a long time, even though I didn't realize it."

"I guess it was a thrill to learn your old home was for sale."

He nodded, then remembered it had been her home, too, for a while. "Does it make you happy to be back?"

She hesitated, and he saw the flat blank look he hated slide over her face yet again. "My memories of living here aren't...that good." She jerked her head in the direction of the outbuildings. "I spent a lot of time in the barn, grooming horses and such."

"Hiding."

She glanced at him. "I suppose so."

"From your father?"

She nodded, one quick, short jerk of the head.

"I'm sorry if it brings back bad memories."

Her head flew up, making her hair dance wildly around her shoulders. "Oh, I don't mind being here now. You've made it a completely different place and I love being here with you—I mean, I love living at the ranch and working for you."

The telephone rang with a shrill br-r-r-ring, interrupting their conversation.

The intrusive noise irritated Cal. He felt as if he'd been on the verge of some meaningful discussion, some irretrievable moment that was gone forever now. Holding Lyn's gaze with his own, he slowly rose as the phone rang a second time, then he reached over and lifted the handset.

"McCall."

"Hello, Cal."

He straightened in his seat, suddenly wary. "Hello, Mother." He sensed Lyn's attention in the way her hands stilled on the rolling pin.

"Cal…" His mother's voice trailed off and he heard her take a deep breath. "I have a favor to ask."

"Ask away," he said without missing a beat. Just because she asked didn't mean he had to do anything he didn't want to.

"I'd like to visit with you while I'm here, if you don't object."

"Of course not." He injected every ounce of courtesy he had in him into his voice. Might as well get it over with. "Would you like to come for dinner?"

"Ah—dinner?" Cora Lee Jenssen sounded startled.

"How about tonight? Lyn's making slippery pot pie. After eating her cooking for a couple of months, I can promise you it will be good."

His mother took another deep breath. "Tonight would be very nice. What time?"

He thought for a minute. "I'll come over and pick you up around six."

"Six. I'll look forward to it."

When he hung up the phone and looked at Lyn, she was industriously rolling out the dough as if she hadn't heard a word he'd said. "My mother's coming for dinner tonight," he told her. "We'll eat about six-thirty, if you can make that work."

She nodded immediately. "Six-thirty is fine. If you like, I'll make something a little more...elegant."

He shook his head. "No, pot pie's fine." *She'll have to take me the way I am if she insists on coming over here.* "And maybe some cookies?"

Lyn laughed. "You're hopeless. All right, I'll make some cookies." As he watched, she doubled the pace at which she was working. "I've got to get this place cleaned up before tonight."

"The house looks fine." He wasn't having her run around like a crazy woman to try to impress his mother.

"Did you leave newspapers on the floor in the den again?" She eyed him suspiciously, ignoring his words.

"Uh, maybe." He took a step back as guilt struck. "I'll go check." Then he turned again and placed both palms flat on the counter. "But you are *not* going to get yourself into a tizz about this. It's just my mother."

She stopped rolling again and stuck out her chin in that stubborn little way she had. He'd already learned what that lifted chin meant. He might as well save his breath as argue with her. When Lyn dug her heels in about something, there was no moving her. "It's your *mother,* Cal," she said. "She's the only one you've got and I'm not going to treat her like one of the hired hands just because you've got some chip on your shoulder about the past."

The words stung. He glowered at her, anger burning a slow fuse inside him.

She glared right back.

Impasse. The good humor and tentative communion were gone.

"Fine." He sliced a hand through the air. "Do whatever you damn well please."

Cal had made it plain that his mother's visit was not to be an occasion, but Lyn refused to treat the evening as if it were nothing special. She knew better than to set the table in the dining room, but she went into the storeroom and brought out a bunch of dried yarrow and several stems of the small shrub roses she'd saved from the summer. She arranged the flower heads in a centerpiece with a fat cinnamon candle in the center. Then, looking critically at her work, she covered the round table in the kitchen with an ivory crocheted cloth and got out the rose cloth napkins that matched the design on the everyday spongewear dishes Silver had picked out.

She got out two bags of pie cherries that a neighbor had sent her last summer and quickly rolled out a one-crust pie bottom. Then she added the cherries and her aunt's ingredients for no-fail cherry pies, interwove fluted-edge strips in a lattice pattern over the top and baked it while she made a broccoli casserole and sliced some carrots to steam. No rolls necessary, since she'd be serving pot pie…hmm, what else should she serve, she wondered.

Soup? A salad? With a twinge of apprehension, she remembered the look in Cal's eye before he'd slammed out the door. Perhaps not. She knew he would never hurt her, but she so rarely saw him in anything but a good humor that an angry Cal made her loath to deliberately provoke him.

She settled for small dishes of homemade applesauce with cinnamon sprinkled over the top. Finally, she rolled a cheese ball in crushed walnuts and placed it, along with crackers, on a spongewear platter.

Her hands were shaking. Nerves. Not for herself, but for Cal. She'd liked Cora Lee Jenssen immensely, had found the lady from Virginia to be the antithesis of a stuck-up woman with too much money. It was clear that Cal resented his mother for leaving him all those years ago, but the woman she'd met wouldn't have done such a thing without a good reason. She wished she could make him understand how precious every day he had with his mother was.

It was five-thirty by the time she finished vacuuming the downstairs, dusting and straightening up, and she quickly ran a mop over the kitchen floor. She'd done it just that morning, but Cal and two of the men had traipsed in and out for drinks and bandages and heaven only knew what else, and they'd left a trail of mud to mark their passage.

Hastily, she ran up to her room and took a quick shower. She braided her hair and caught it up with pins in a knot at the back of her neck, sprayed herself with scent and then put on one of the few nice blouses she owned with her newest pair of jeans. It was at times like this that she felt most keenly her lack of sophistication. She didn't even own a casual skirt or a pair of pants other than jeans!

Looking in the mirror over her dresser, she shook her head critically. The closest thing she possessed to makeup was a tinted lip gloss, which she applied. The scar across her jaw had continued to fade as the plastic surgeon had assured her it would, but there was still an obvious hitch marring the line of her lip on that side.

Slowly, she put her fingers up to the scar, running them along the ridge of scar tissue she still could feel. She rarely thought about the physical damage that had been done to her anymore. But now she wondered. Who had hit her? What kind of weapon had caused a long scar like that? A fist might have split her lip but it wouldn't have left that kind of tear.

In her mind's eye, a knife flashed!

It was a pocketknife, but the blade was sharp, just the same. She'd told him to get out or she'd call the police and that's when he'd pulled the knife.

She backed away from him, afraid to take her eyes off that knife.

"Bitch. I want money and I want it now!" Wayne lunged and grabbed her by the arm. "I have to have money."

He struck her with his fists, kicked her in the ribs and knocked the breath right out of her. Before she could recover, he had his hands around her throat, squeezing until she couldn't draw a breath. She swore to herself that if she lived through this, Wayne Galloway was going to prison. Her vision was dimming; instinctively she jerked her knee up, catching him squarely in the groin. His eyes widened in shock and pain and he made an agonized groaning sound as he doubled over and dropped to his knees.

She had to get out, get away. She staggered to her feet and edged past the man writhing on the floor. The door was less than fifteen feet away. If she could get out of the apartment, she could—

His hand curled around her ankle and yanked her foot from under her, and she went down hard on her side. He was on her in a minute, still screaming about money. She fought him, and at some point during the struggle he got the knife up to her face.

She saw it coming, like a slow-motion replay of an accident. The blade descended—

And she got her hand up in time to knock it away. But she didn't knock it far enough. A thin line of fire sliced across her jaw and down her neck. He'd cut her! A strength she didn't know she had burst forth; she reared up and shoved him, hard. He went over backward and hit his head on the corner of the table—

My God. She stared at herself in the mirror. She really had done it. She'd killed Wayne. One hand was stuffed against her mouth in denial and she forced herself to loosen the taut muscles. My God. She was a murderess.

The other memory fragment floated into her head. Who had the other man been? She'd been hiding in a closet when he'd banged on the door—hiding from Wayne. Had this happened before or after Wayne had pulled the knife on her? It *had* to have happened before if he'd died when he struck his head on the table. Or had it?

A small ray of hope, weak but steady, shone through her dark thoughts. Maybe that fall hadn't killed him.

One thing she knew for sure, *she* hadn't been the one to stuff his body into a closet to rot. The mere thought made her want to gag.

Then an old board squeaked in the hallway, and she jumped halfway to the ceiling at the unexpected sound.

Cal's footsteps passed her door and she heard the steps creak beneath his weight. She glanced at her watch and realized he'd be going to get his mother any minute. Oh, Lord! She'd better get down there and check on dinner.

She hurried from her room and rushed down the stairs to the kitchen. As she rounded the corner from the hallway, Cal stood blocking her way. He held the phone in one hand, but as she barreled into him he put out his free arm and caught her, splaying his fingers wide on her spine and holding her against his big, warm frame when she would have moved away.

Over her head, she heard him conclude a conversation with another rancher. She stirred once, pushing at him, but it was like pushing at a bull that had braced his legs. He didn't even indicate that he'd noticed, except to tighten his arm around her waist, and she closed her eyes momentarily in despair. Her pulse raced as his hard strength registered and the musky male scent he wore teased her nostrils, increasing her longing for him to an almost unbearable pitch.

"You bet, George. I'll see you at the sale barn then."

Cal hit the off button on the mobile phone and set it down on the counter. He leaned back a fraction and looked at her with raised eyebrows. "Well, look what I caught. What are you in such an all-fired hurry for?"

She couldn't think straight when he held her like this. She was supremely conscious of the steely strength of his arm around her back, the heat of his unyielding body, the warm, smoky good humor in his gaze. "I—I, uh…"

"Whatever you say." His lips curved into a lazy grin, and her heart jumped as strong white teeth flashed. He knew he'd flustered her. Then he turned fully to face her, sliding his body against her until she was lodged firmly against his chest. Her legs brushed his and his hips pressed into her belly.

Her knees felt like jelly. Deep in her quivering abdomen, a fist clenched and she sucked in a breath of much-needed air.

"I told myself I wasn't going to do this." Cal muttered the words as his head came down and she felt moist searing breath against the sensitive skin of her neck. "But I can't seem to convince myself it's a bad idea." His lips slid across her cheek and hovered above hers. "Tell me it's a bad idea."

She shook her head the tiniest bit without speaking, lifting her chin while she kept her eyes on his. Loving him as she did, she couldn't turn him away, didn't *want* to turn him away. She slipped her palms up his broad chest to his wide shoulders in mute appeal.

Cal made a sound deep in his throat, a groan of pleasure, and his hands clasped her hips with almost bruising force. He took her mouth in a deep, searching kiss, his tongue sliding easily between her lips and flirting with her teeth until she opened for him and met his ardor with her own. The kiss went on and on and she felt his big body shaking against hers. Or maybe it was her shaking against him. Who cared? Then she felt the slightest withdrawal as he lessened the intensity of the kiss.

"I have to go," he murmured against her mouth. His lips continued to mold hers with decreasing pressure until he was merely brushing his mouth over hers. "We need to talk later."

She nodded, drawing in a shaky breath as he set her to one side and reached for the keys on the hook at the side of the cabinets.

"Now remember," he said, and his voice was suddenly cooler, harsher, distant. "We're not making a big fuss about my mother visiting. This is just another meal. Got it?"

She nodded, but he was already striding out the door. "Got it."

How could he do that, she wondered? How could he turn off the passion so easily? He'd been as aroused and affected as she had by that kiss, she was sure of it. In all her life, Lyn had never known she could feel like this. Instinctively, she recognized that Cal was the man of whom she would dream for the rest of her life, the man she had been made for, the only man she could ever come alive for again.

It wasn't fair that such feelings could be one-sided.

Then again, she thought with a slightly bitter resignation, when had her life ever been fair? Some people just weren't made to live their dreams.

"Well, duh," she said aloud as she realized how pathetic and self-pitying her thoughts were. She was grateful that her life was as good as it was right now. She was never hungry, never cold, never fearful that she'd anger someone and get slapped. No one took her paychecks or locked her in her room. Her present was pretty darn good compared to her past. Why make herself miserable wishing for a future that wasn't going to happen?

She turned and slapped both hands on the counter. She just had time to feed the dogs and cats before Cal returned with his mother.

Dinner was a success in her eyes. Cal's mother was as sweet as she'd been at their first meeting, chatting easily with Lyn and working to draw Cal into the conversation. She praised the food and talked about her own mother's recipe for deep-dish pot pie, promising to send it to Lyn once she returned to Virginia.

Lyn caught Cal's narrowed look when she brought out the cherry pie along with the plate of raisin cookies she'd baked for him. She knew exactly what he was thinking. *Don't do anything special.*

Well, the heck with him. If making a few desserts qualified as something special, then so be it.

The meal went smoothly. But then, she'd expected it to. Cal was courteous to a fault, never letting the conversation flag and playing the part of the host flawlessly. Cora Lee Jenssen was too well-bred to make a scene, but Lyn wondered if she longed to scream at him as badly as Lyn did. She could see the hurt and despair in his mother's eyes, watched the woman grow quieter and quieter as Cal moved the conversation from one meaningless topic to another throughout the meal.

He insisted Lyn join them for coffee afterward in the living room, no doubt so he wouldn't have to spend any significant time alone with his parent. By the time the evening ended and Cal asked his mother if she'd like him to drive her back to Silver's, Lyn could almost see the tears the older woman was holding in check. She finished cleaning the kitchen while he was gone, banging pots and pans around in an unsatisfying cacophony of clashing sounds, wishing she could bang some sense into Cal's thick head.

He walked into the kitchen just in time to see her slam the pantry door.

"Whoa!" he said. "Did something happen while I was gone?"

"No." She ignored him and concentrated on wiping down the table.

He eyed her for a minute. "You were smiling when I left here. Now you look like you'd like to take a bite out of someone. Want to tell me why?"

Lyn threw the dishcloth onto the table. "Why? *Why?*" She crossed her arms and gave him an accusatory, unflinching stare. "Why did you bother inviting your mother to dinner tonight?"

His eyes narrowed, and she could see a curtain drop over his thoughts as surely as if he'd physically withdrawn from the room. "Because she called and indicated she'd like to visit. *If* you recall."

"And you call this evening a visit." Her voice was scornful. "You went out of your way to make that poor woman feel like a casual acquaintance whom you were obligated to entertain."

"I was polite!" he said through clenched teeth.

"That you were," she agreed. "Would you like an award?"

Cal spun and stalked the length of the kitchen and back again. He ran a hand through his hair in a gesture that betrayed his discomfort. "'That poor woman' *is* a casual acquaintance," he said, and she heard defensiveness in his tone. "I saw her once a year during my childhood. I barely know her."

"She's trying to remedy that!"

"I don't care!" The words were a shout, echoing through the old house's cozy rooms.

Lyn stared at him in astonishment. Cal wasn't one to lose his temper; she could count on one hand the times she'd seen him angry, and she'd never seen his composure slip like this.

"You should care," she said quietly. She picked up the dishcloth and slowly crossed to the sink, then turned to face him again. "My father treated me like a servant. As far back as I can remember, he expected me to keep his house, clean his clothes, make his meals. I never remember having any sense of kinship. If he loved me, he did a darn good job of hiding it."

"It's a different situation. You don't know anything about my mother and me."

"I know that she wants to be a part of your life now," she said. "I know that she loves you. I know that you're hurting her—you know it, too, and you don't care."

They stared at each other across the kitchen, but Lyn could feel the chasm between them yawning much, much wider. "Never mind," she said stiffly. "It isn't any of my business. I'm just the hired help." She turned her back on him, rinsing and wringing out the dishcloth, and all the while she could feel her heart being wrung and twisted, as well. She *knew* Cal was a loving, caring man. *Why* couldn't he extend that compassion to his mother?

Cal didn't contradict her last words. He simply stood, big hands at his sides, watching her through angry eyes as she walked out of the kitchen and headed for the stairs. She could almost feel the waves of hostility emanating from him, and the fist around her heart squeezed even tighter.

"Good night," she said quietly.

He didn't answer.

Hours later, she was still awake, waiting for his familiar footsteps on the stairs. But he hadn't come to bed when she finally fell into a troubled sleep in the wee hours of the morning.

Three days later, Cal eyed the rigid line of Lyn's back as she walked across the yard to where he had the stock trailer hitched to the truck. He was taking a couple of dry cows to the sale barn over in Philip today, and Lyn had asked if she could ride along to do some shopping.

It was going to be a damned long drive, if the silence of the past couple days was any indication.

The way he got along with his mother was *his* affair,

he told himself for at least the hundredth time. He'd been a good host. What more could she ask? He ignored the little voice in his head that prodded at his guilty conscience, the mental pictures of his mother's sad eyes. He owed her *nothing,* dammit! He didn't even have to invite her into his home, and he had. He'd been perfectly friendly and scrupulously polite. After the way she'd abandoned him, he thought his behavior was pretty magnanimous.

So what in hell was he thinking about it for? That was ancient history.

He followed Lyn to the truck and climbed into the driver's seat. "You ready?"

She nodded. Just nodded. Didn't even bother to speak. As snooty as she'd been, it wouldn't have surprised him if she'd written a note to ask him about riding along. Then she wouldn't have had to speak to him at all.

He was right. It was the longest forty minutes he'd ever spent in a truck. And possibly the chilliest, too. He dropped her off on Pine Street in front of the variety store.

"Thank you," she said, never meeting his eyes as she slid out of the truck. "I'll walk over to the sale barn and meet you when I'm done."

Three hours later, the auction was winding down. He stood with one booted foot against the wall in the very back of the tiered seating area, watching the bidding on a big three-year-old black gelding that was dead lame. He was reasonably pleased with the price his cows had brought. Absently, he eyed the horse again. Too bad it was lame. It was a good-looking piece of horseflesh. His father had owned horses trained by the same fella who broke this one, and Cal still remembered how well they'd handled. Breaking colts was a gift. Some people were better at it than others. He'd always preferred to buy horses that had been broken by someone who knew what they were doing. Absently, he wondered what had become of the horse that had been his during his youth, when Lyn appeared at his elbow.

"Hey," he said, wondering if shopping had worked any of the kinks out of her recent attitude. "Want to get some lunch?"

"Can you buy that gelding?" She pointed at the sale board and he heard excitement in her voice. "He's going to the processing plant if you don't."

"No. Look, he's lame." He pointed to the horse's hobbling gait. "Too bad. I'd have liked to have bought another Triple Creek horse."

"I looked at him outside," she said in an urgent whisper. "The guy selling him says he thinks it's navicular disease, but I'm pretty sure it's an abscess back near the heel. I borrowed a pair of tongs from the vet and checked. I can heal it, Cal; I know I can."

He took his eye off the horse and stared at her, wondering how far he should trust her judgment. Navicular disease was an erosion of the bone that couldn't be cured, and the horse would have to be put down anyway. On the other hand, an abscess could be cured with a hoof knife, some soaking and antibiotics in the right hands. Lyn wasn't one to offer opinions idly. She had a good touch with the animals that needed healing at the ranch. And she'd worked for veterinarians for several years....what the hell. He raised his bid card.

Two minutes later he was the proud owner of a lame gelding that he hadn't intended to buy in the first place. "You'd better be right about this," he told her.

She nodded. "I am." Then she placed her hand on his forearm and squeezed it lightly. "Thank you. I couldn't bear to see that horse destroyed. He'll make you a good cowhorse.'' Her eyes were a deep mossy green and her cheeks were pink from her walk in the cool air; she looked about as delectable as any woman he'd ever seen, and his pulse hammered as his body reacted to her nearness. He couldn't even recall why he'd been annoyed with her.

''You're welcome.'' As usual, her lush, wide mouth drew his attention. He had more fantasies about those full lips on his body than he could even remember any more. The urge to slide his arm around her and pull her to him for a thorough kiss was strong, and for a moment, the air around them seemed to still and thicken to a frozen instant in time. Her breasts rose and fell as she took several shallow breaths and his gaze dropped lower, to where the soft flesh made gentle mounds beneath her denim jacket. His body stirred and he hastily dragged his attention back to her face. The jeans he was wearing weren't going to hide anything and he'd be damned if he'd have all the ranchers hanging around here today snickering about McCall and his...his what? Household help didn't exactly define Lyn's place in his life anymore.

''Hello, folks.'' A hearty slap on the back would have made him stagger if he was a smaller man, and he turned to see Marty Stryker grinning at them both.

''Hi, Marty.'' Lyn seemed pleased to see him and Cal felt his hackles rising at the familiar way Marty slipped his arm around her waist and kissed her cheek.

''You still hanging out with this fool?'' he asked her. ''Just say the word and I'll whisk you away from your life of servitude. We could be married tomorrow.''

Lyn laughed, and the husky music touched a chord in his chest that traveled straight to his groin. He shifted uncomfortably as she said, "Sure, Marty. And of course, if I married you, I would live a life of luxury."

"You would, sweet thing." Marty's sky-blue eyes twinkled. "The only small favor I'd ask is that you be a mother to my daughter. Cheyenne's a quiet, well-behaved child. You'd barely know she was around."

Cal snorted at the mention of Marty's wild child as Lyn hooted. "Do you have Irish ancestors?" she asked. "Because you sure know how to spin a tale."

Marty laughed, too. "How come nobody falls for that line?" He reached for the double doors that led to the front hallway. "I'm going to have some lunch before I head home. You guys want to join me?"

Five minutes ago, lunch with Lyn had been at the top of his agenda. Now, however, he was anxious to get going. To have her to himself again. "Sorry," he said to Marty. "I just bought a horse and I want to get him home."

Marty shrugged. "No problem. Lyn can eat with me and then I'll drop her by your place on my way home."

There was a small silence. Lyn looked at the dusty concrete floor rather than at Cal. "I have to stop by the pharmacy before I leave," she said. "Is that a problem?"

Marty shook his head. "Not at all." He crooked his elbow and offered her his arm. "Your meal awaits," he said to her. He grinned over the top of her head at Cal. "See you later, buddy."

He was so frustrated he had to grit his teeth as he watched Marty turn and walk away with Lyn. Damn that sneak! No way was he going to let Lyn marry Marty. Everybody knew how desperate the man was to find a woman to keep his household and his kid in line. Lyn had had enough of men dictating her life—he wasn't going to have Marty trying to be the next one.

Noble of you.

Silver entrusted me with Lyn's welfare when she came to work for me, he told the mocking voice in his head. *I'm just looking out for what's best for her.*

So kissing the girl silly and then picking a fight is how you look out for her?

Well, hell. There was no answer for that one. In a filthier mood than he'd been in when he arrived, he stomped out of the sale barn through the sloppy parking lot and pulled his trailer around to pick up the horse he hadn't planned to buy.

Six

Lyn waved as Marty backed his truck around and left the yard. She'd had a pleasant afternoon catching up on the latest local gossip with him, though she'd had a moment of bitter disappointment at the sale barn when Cal had abandoned her to Marty's invitation.

So what had she expected? He'd been surly as a bull since the night his mother had eaten with them. She knew she'd overstepped her bounds. She was just his employee. It was none of her business how he and his mother got along.

Even if he had kissed her senseless twice in the past week.

For the twentieth time, she cautioned herself not to read too much into those kisses. Cal hadn't dated another woman since he'd been in Kadoka. She probably looked good to him solely because she was the lone female in his life day after day.

Still, she *had* looked good to him, at least a little. And she was still trying to get up her nerve to let him know it was all right for him to…to enjoy her body if he wanted her. He'd given her so much that she'd do anything to repay him.

The weather had turned downright cold and a hefty wind was blowing; a light snow was whirling around and she'd heard they were supposed to get maybe a foot. She shivered as she took her purchases indoors but she came out again immediately and headed for the barn. She couldn't wait to see the new horse.

Cal had put him in the roomiest stall. She walked clear up to the rail before she realized Cal was inside with the gelding.

"Hello," she said, feeling awkward. She remembered the look in his eyes when she'd agreed to stay in town with Marty. "How's he doing?"

Cal grunted. "Settling in fine. The leg doesn't look very good, though."

"Let me see." She frowned and opened the door, slipping into the stall and rubbing the horse's velvety nose after he'd inspected her. She moved to his side and lifted the gelding's leg, checking the suspected abscess carefully. After a moment she looked at Cal. "If you'll hold him, I'll cut it down and let it start draining," she said. "He really should be on an antibiotic, too."

"I picked up some before I came home." Cal tossed a bottle at her. "Figured you'd want to get him straightened out right away."

She barely caught the big plastic bottle with both hands. "Thank you."

"I did it for the horse." His voice was surly.

It seemed there was little she could say that wouldn't irritate him so she didn't say anything more, just gathered antiseptic cleanser, a hoof knife and other things she would need. They worked in silence, except for occasional soothing murmurs to the gelding and the rising howl of the wind as it brought the snow. Finally she rose. "I was sure it was an abscess. You'll be able to start working him before you know it."

Cal muttered something she didn't catch as she cleaned up and gave the horse the first antibiotic, but when she started for the house he was at her side.

The wind was screaming around them as Cal pushed open the heavy barn door. She started forward right behind him, but just then a capricious blast wrested the door from Cal's grasp and sent it slamming shut—right on her.

Her breath whooshed out and she saw stars as the door caught her directly between her breasts and pinned her against the frame. Too stunned to figure out exactly what had happened, she tried to gasp for air and couldn't. Pressure squeezed her chest; she opened her mouth to cry out but no sound came forth. Her arms flailed; she couldn't get a grip on the edge of the door, though it would have been useless in any case. The wind had to be blowing around seventy miles an hour. Combined with the weight of the door, there was no way she could move it.

In the next instant, Cal yanked the door away. She started to slide to the floor but he was there, swinging her into his arms and shouting an order at one of the hands who'd appeared. "Shut that goddamn door!"

He jolted her as he ran full out across the yard and into the mudroom, and she groaned as her desperate lungs filled with a necessary breath of air.

"God, baby, I'm sorry, oh, God." Cal laid her on the braided rug and started working on the buttons of her jacket. "Can you talk? How bad is it?"

"I'm—okay." She wheezed, but as her breathing steadied she found her voice again. "I think I'm okay."

"Any pain in your legs?" He ran his hands down each of her legs from hip to toe, his fingers probing.

"No." She struggled to sit up, to reassure him. "It didn't hurt me badly. Scared me silly, though."

He held her upright and stripped the jacket away, then pressed her back again and started on the buttons of her flannel shirt. His big fingers fumbled repeatedly, and after a moment he muttered a vivid curse. Then, before she knew what was happening, he took the front of the shirt in both hands and ripped it apart. Buttons flew.

She gasped, and this time it wasn't because she couldn't breathe. "Cal!" Her hands flew up to encircle his wrists.

His rough fingers unclasped the front hook on her bra. Her restraining hands barely slowed his progress; for all the notice he gave, she might as well have saved her energy. Then he folded back the edges of the shirt, and she realized with gratitude that he'd been careful not to expose her nipples. It was a silly thing, but she felt slightly less bare. His index finger traced a gentle path down the midline of her body. "You're going to bruise."

She stopped moving, stopped trying to tug his hands away. The sensation of his callused finger on her skin was an exquisite torture. Compared to the shimmering excitement coursing through her, the minor dull ache of the bruising barely registered.

"I'm sorry," he said, his gaze lifting to meet hers. "The wind tore that door right out of my hand. I wasn't expecting it—" He stopped and bowed his head, and a shudder ran through his big body. "God, you could have been hurt badly."

She couldn't bear to see him so distressed. "It wasn't

your fault.'' She raised herself on her elbows, wincing a little as she inspected the six-inch red line streaking down her breastbone. She'd seen worse. She sat up, forgetting her discomfort. ''Cal, it wasn't your fault,'' she repeated. She put her hands on his shoulders and massaged lightly, then leaned forward and laid her cheek against his hair. ''It was an accident. I'm not hurt badly.'' She chuckled. ''And I should know.''

He stirred then, lifting his head, and she realized with jolt that their faces were only inches apart. His eyes were shielded from her gaze; he was looking down at her body again, and the sight of the long, dark eyelashes lying against his cheek brought a strange intimacy to the moment. Something softened and stirred in her belly, and she shivered.

Then he lifted his hands, slipped them inside her opened shirt around her rib cage just above her waist. His hands were so big his fingers nearly met around her slender frame, and his thumbs lightly rubbed up and down, sliding almost to the underswell of her breasts with each stroke.

It was as if he never heard her reassurances. ''I'm sorry,'' he said again, so quietly that she could barely hear him. He bent slowly and leaned forward, pressing his lips to her flesh directly between her breasts where the red mark was already showing purple mottling. ''Your skin is so beautiful,'' he whispered, brushing featherlight kisses against her. ''Like warm satin.''

Her hands slid from his shoulders up the column of his strong neck and into his hair, gripping the thick strands in an involuntary shiver of pleasure. ''Cal,'' she whispered.

He stilled for a moment. She almost stopped breathing, sure that he was going to draw away, and her disappointment of earlier in the day was nothing compared to the bitter regret she felt now.

Then he moved again—

And instead of moving away, his mouth moved slowly, purposefully over the rise of one breast until she felt him tug her nipple into his mouth with a gentle suckling.

She whimpered as great waves of sexual arousal shot through her, swamping her awareness of everything but Cal and his clever hands and seeking mouth. She held his mouth to her breast, arching her back and pushing herself at him. Never in her whole life had she felt as she felt now, and she cradled his head in her arms, pressing kisses against his hair.

He lifted his head then, sliding his palm up to cup the breast he'd abandoned as he sought her mouth. She lifted her face to his, meeting his lips with a soft moan that made his big body tremble. He speared the fingers of his other hand through her hair and tilted her face even more, dropping quick, urgent kisses over her cheeks and eyelids and forehead and nose before coming back to drink deeply from her mouth again.

When he lifted his head, they were both panting.

"What am I doing?" He grinned crookedly. "I mean, I know *what* I'm doing, believe me, but why am I doing it? You've just been smashed in a barn door. You need—"

She stopped his words simply, by pressing her mouth to his. "You," she whispered against his lips. "I need *you.*"

He drew back a fraction. "You aren't afraid...you know, of being with a man?"

"You're the only man I've thought of being with." She looked into his eyes. "And I could never be afraid of you."

He hesitated, and fear chilled her. Was he going to stop?

Then her fears evaporated and she closed her eyes as his strong arms flexed, drawing her closer as his mouth began to move against hers again with masterful purpose. He drew her to her knees against him and she could feel the hard ridge of his arousal behind his jeans as he pressed against her body. "Maybe you should be," he said, but there was a smile in his voice, and in response, she rolled her hips against him.

He groaned then and tore his mouth from hers, and her eyes flew open. He helped her to her feet, and she stood uncertainly as he turned away from her, but he only took a moment to lock the back door. Then he was with her again, tearing open the buttons of his shirt and shucking out of it before ripping his T-shirt over his head. He gathered her to him, leaning back a little, and she shivered at the gleam in his hooded gaze as he surveyed her flesh uncovered by the shirt he'd torn open. He pushed the edges of the material back and gently pulled her against him, and she inhaled sharply as the sensitive tips of her breasts crushed against the hard-muscled planes of his. He slowly rubbed back and forth against her nipples. The tender peaks drew into taut little points at the sensual contact. He smiled at the sight, rasping his thumbs across them, moving in steady circles, stroking and tugging with just the right amount of pressure until an unending river of sensation streamed from her breasts to her womb and she was rocking restlessly against him.

After a moment, he dropped his hands and unfastened her jeans, kneeling to pull off her boots before he began to work the pants down her legs, stopping to stroke and explore the tender skin as he went. She nearly screamed when his tongue found the backs of her knees. He moved higher, kissing a path up her thighs and finally nipping at the edge of her practical cotton panties. He pressed a kiss to her *there,* his breath searing her through the cloth, and she arched upward. No one had ever done that to her before; she was totally unprepared for the heavy surge of sensation that quickly followed as he flicked his tongue against her. Her hips lifted, pressing her harder against his mouth, and she whimpered.

He came to his feet then, looming over her slighter frame, pulling her to him and kissing her deeply while he pushed her opened shirt off her shoulders and down her arms to the floor. One hand stroked her body: her breasts, her waist, her hips, down her buttocks and up the gentle crease between, sliding around to part her legs gently and slipping his hand between them. He cupped her, using his thumb to play her senses, and she couldn't believe he hadn't even removed her panties yet.

As if he could read her mind, he stepped back a pace and his hands moved to the fragile barrier, whisking them down her legs and tossing them aside. He stood stock-still for a moment, taking in every inch of her pale flesh. Then he slowly slid his palm down her belly, moving steadily until he'd tangled the fingers of one hand in the dark red curls at the junction of her legs, and his breath grew short.

Suddenly he was fumbling with his belt, ripping at his pants and shoving them out of the way. She gulped in one shocked breath of air as the full power of his proud male shaft reared against his belly. It had been a long time, but she knew her husband had never been so...well-proportioned. A tiny stab of doubt shot through her, and she raised her gaze to his.

"I'm not sure this is going to work," she said, hearing the tremor in her voice.

Cal smiled down at her, his eyes blazing with the heat of his need. "I am," he said in a deep growl. He took her by the hips and tugged her against him, letting her feel his strong, eager flesh against her while he sought her mouth yet again, and despite her newfound worry, the spark of desire that he so easily lit within her raced through her until she was consumed by it once again. She rocked herself back and forth against him, loving the hard silky heat of him trapped between their bodies, rubbing over him while his tongue showed her what he wanted and his fingers stroked her breasts in rhythm with the movements of their hips.

He slipped a hand across her hip and inward, moving her thigh wider. Then she felt his fingers probing, seeking, testing her most private parts, and she could feel the humid moisture rising to his touch. He began to rub a light circular pattern and she gasped, her legs shaking a little, her fingers blindly flexing in the mat of dark hair covering his chest, and he made a hoarse sound against her mouth.

"*Now,*" he growled.

He lifted her with his hands at her waist until he snuggled between her thighs and she felt the slick, hot tip of him pushing at her. She wriggled herself against him, helping him enter her and then, as he slowly flexed his hips, she buried her face against his shoulder to muffle the sound of her cries. He filled her and filled her until she was sure he couldn't fill her any more, and then he let go of her waist, clasping her buttocks in his big hands and tilting her hips a fraction, and she realized with a start that he *could* fill her more.

"That's it, baby. Take me. All of me." Cal's voice was unrecognizable, deep and strained as he propped himself against the edge of the dryer and braced his legs and she automatically twined her limbs around his. She had a moment's incredulous reaction as she recalled that they were in the *mudroom* and then she couldn't think at all. She slid her hands over taut, hard muscle and clutched his shoulders. His hands clasped her bottom and he held her to him, his mouth taking hers as he began to thrust his hips in an age-old rhythm. She felt every tiny motion, from the rough rub of his hair against her to the glide and drag of his hot flesh moving in and out of her, and a rushing, heady excitement flowered within her. His hips hammered at her, pounding an ever-increasing drum-roll, and each time their hips met, the fresh shock of the connection shoved her higher and higher. Cal tore his mouth from hers, throwing his head back, his teeth bared in a grimace as he gave himself to the moment. His breathing was hoarse and wild, his chest heaving like a bellows.

She was gasping for air, too, and their bodies were slick and hot with the sweat of their exertions. Her body drew taut as she spiraled wildly toward the peak, and suddenly she was there, her body heaving and shaking as her womb fisted and her muscles repeatedly spasmed. Cal made an animal sound deep in his throat and his hands became a vise, holding her writhing body in place as he went rigid, his hips pumping while he poured himself into her. She could feel the hot essence of him against her inner walls as she began to calm, and slowly his frantic finish ended, leaving him slumped against the dryer with her curled bonelessly on his chest, arms looped around his neck.

Finally his hands dropped from her hips and dangled at his sides. "Good God," he muttered. "Did we survive?"

For some reason that struck her funny. She began to

giggle helplessly, laughing harder as he took her shoulders and drew her back so that he could look quizzically into her face. Then he shifted, straightening, and she stopped laughing abruptly. Within her, he was as full and ready as if the past minutes had never happened. He put his hands beneath her bottom, then stood for a moment, looking around. "Ah, *hell.*"

"What's wrong?" His sudden bad humor drained the pleasure she'd been feeling.

He looked at her wryly, then shook his head, and she relaxed as she realized he was chuckling. "I was going to walk right through the house to my bedroom with you just like this."

"Um." She smiled and ducked her head, ridiculously feeling shy. "Sounds good to me."

"I can't," he said. "My pants are around my ankles but I can't kick them off because I'm still wearing my boots."

She looked down, another bubble of laughter rising as she saw his predicament. Then he lifted her off him regretfully, yanking up the offending garments while she gathered scattered clothing. He put a hand on her arm and she turned to him, but he didn't speak, only lifted her into his arms and carried her through the house and upstairs to the huge bed in his room, where he stripped back the covers and gently lay her down. He took the clothes from her and tossed them carelessly on the floor, then sat on the bed to remove his boots before finally taking off his jeans.

Lyn lay quietly the whole time, watching the play of hard-packed muscle in his back, the bunch of powerful arms and the rock-hard power of his thighs. He couldn't hide the fact that he wanted her again, and she wordlessly held out her arms when he turned toward her, inviting him into her embrace. Offering him her love though she couldn't tell him so.

This time, his lovemaking was less frantic. He stroked and explored and caressed every inch of her, then lay back and let her do the same, clenching handfuls of the sheet in his big fists when her hands came to the thatch of dark hair cushioning him, groaning and arching his hips helplessly when she finally stroked his taut, silky flesh with a tentative hand. He rolled over onto her, pressing her into the mattress with his big body and entering her, then lingered over their union, rocking the bed with smooth, strong strokes that never increased in pace but lit the now-familiar fire within her all the same. When she convulsed in his arms, it triggered his release, and he stiffened against her until his body finally relaxed and he lay over her, chest heaving.

"Am I too heavy?" His voice was muffled in the pillow just above her head.

"No." She shook her head, wrapping her arms around him to hold him in place. Her breastbone ached a little where the bruise was developing, but she didn't remind him. She never wanted this moment to end. He was still snugly nestled within her and they'd been as intimate as two people could be. She'd never been happier in her life.

Finally, he lifted his head. He grunted as he slid away from her, but he only reached down to drag the covers over them, then gathered her into his arms and lay back with her cuddled against his side. Her head was pillowed on his arm and her cheek pressed against his chest.

She didn't speak. She didn't really know what to say, and she was afraid words would spoil the magic in the moment.

Finally, he sighed and spoke. "I was pretty damn mad

at Marty this morning when he horned in on our lunch date.''

She smiled, smoothing a hand over the ridged muscles of his abdomen. "I don't care for Marty except as a friend."

He was silent.

She considered her last words, then wondered if they had been too much of a declaration. After all, he hadn't said anything about emotion. For him, this was a physical thing.

"I mean," she said awkwardly, trying to minimize the damage, "you're the one who's been so kind to me. I can never repay you for the way you've helped me get my life back together. I've wanted to tell you for a long time that I'd do anything..." She stopped when Cal's muscles grew taut and hard as iron beneath her. This wasn't coming out quite the way she'd intended.

Suddenly, he pulled away from her, sitting up in the bed and staring at her. His brows were a straight dark line. "Are you telling me," he said in an ominously quiet, even tone, "that you slept with me just now because *you think you owe me?*"

"It wasn't like that." But her voice lacked conviction as guilt struck her. Hadn't she been thinking of doing exactly that?

"No?" His voice sounded furious, and a shiver of foreboding ran down her spine.

She sat up, too, drawing the sheet to her breasts. "Cal, I—"

"You just told me you've been expecting this all along. Every time I touched you, every damned time I kissed you, you were thinking, 'Gee, I guess it's payback time.'" He threw back the sheets and stood, crossing to the window and leaning his hands heavily on the sill. "I don't know what I thought was happening here, Lyn, but *it sure as hell wasn't gratitude!*" The words grew to a shout and despite herself, she shrank back. Logically, she knew Cal would never hurt her, but she'd been shouted at before and it was hard to change old patterns, old reactions. "Consider your debt paid in full," he said. "A couple rounds of sex in exchange for a little human kindness."

"I—"

"Put your clothes on and get out of here," he said, his voice as rough and angry as she'd ever heard it. His breathing was harsh and loud in the silence; his fists were clenched at his sides.

She sat frozen in place, trying to figure out what to do, how to salvage the wreckage of what had been the most beautiful day of her entire life.

"*Get out!*"

She jumped, practically leaping out of the bed and grabbing her clothing, running from the room without stopping to dress. She rushed down the hallway to her own room, racing in and slamming the door. The clothing slipped from her hands as she stood in the middle of the room. Her nakedness felt wrong now, and she hurriedly threw on the bulky flannel robe Cal's sister had given her.

Cal's sister...*Cal.* How could this have turned out so badly? Tears stung her eyes. She was stupid. She should have known better. What man would want to be told he'd gotten sex as a thank-you gift? She had no idea what Cal *was* thinking, but that certainly had pushed every button he had. She'd offended the only man in the world who meant anything to her, and at the thought that he might ask her to leave, she broke down completely.

She threw herself across her bed and sobbed until her

voice was hoarse and her eyes felt so swollen she could barely see. She must have fallen into an exhausted stupor after that because when she raised her head it was almost full dark. She glanced at the clock and was shocked to see that it was a full hour after the normal suppertime, and she rolled to her feet slowly, dragging herself downstairs to see if Cal was hungry. And if she still had a job.

He wasn't in the office or the living room or the kitchen, but there was a note on the counter in his distinctive block lettering. *Eating at the city bar. Will need a lunch packed tomorrow. C.*

She picked the note up and turned it over as if she expected it to say more. But the back was blank. He hadn't told her to pack her things, only his lunch. He hadn't fired her. Yet, she reminded herself.

She picked at a bite of chicken and had a bowl of applesauce, then fed the animals and checked on the black gelding, who appeared to be settling in well. He came right to her, nuzzling his soft, velvety nose against her cheek and blowing out softly in contentment when she produced a carrot. After that, she trudged into the house and up the stairs to her room, where she got ready for bed. Tears stung her eyes again as she thought of the way Cal had misinterpreted her lovemaking, and she fell into a deep, dull sleep.

She woke in the middle of the night, disoriented. Had she heard something? She sat up and looked toward the window, knowing there was still fire danger from the dry year they were having.

Then a large shadow moved in the doorway. "Hey, there."

Her heart banged painfully against her ribs. "Hi."

Cal cleared his throat. "I, uh, I'm sorry for shouting at you earlier."

The words vibrated through her, breaking up her depression, and she smiled in the dark. "It's all right. I didn't mean—"

"It doesn't matter."

He crossed the room and lifted the covers, sliding into bed beside her, and she realized with a shock that he was naked. His hard, warm body slid against hers and he gathered her gently into his arms as if she were breakable. "Do you want me?" It was a rough, deep whisper.

She turned her face into the hollow of his throat, her arms encircling his neck and gripping fiercely. "Yes," she said against his skin. His flesh was warm beneath her mouth, roughened by hair, and she dragged her open mouth across his collarbone. "Yes," she said again.

His arms slid beneath her and he turned her onto her back, moving with her so that his whole length was sprawled over her. One hairy leg pushed between hers, opening her thighs wide, and he settled himself between them. He was heavily aroused, pressing snugly against her belly, and she felt him pulsing with need.

He propped himself above her on his elbows and used his thumbs to wipe away her tears. "I hurt you. I'm sorry."

Her lips trembled as she smiled up at him. "It's all right."

He shook his head, framing her face with his fingers. "No. None of this is all right. But I can't stay away from you anymore."

"I don't want you to stay away." She almost blurted it out then. *I love you.* But she caught the words back. Cal didn't want her love, just her passion. Instead, she slipped her palms down his back to the crease of his buttocks, slowly slipping her fingers along the groove to the joint where his legs met.

"I can't wait," he warned her. His teeth nipped her shoulder as he drew back and she felt his hand sliding over her breasts, her belly, the slight rise of her pubis, and then a strong finger found the pleated folds between her legs. He probed and pressed until she yielded and then he drew away, guiding himself into position while he supported himself above her on one muscled arm.

Her breath caught painfully in her chest as she felt him, blunt, hot, hard, poised, pushing through her, into her, filling her so completely that she grasped his shoulders in sudden shock. "Stop! It's too much."

He chuckled, part laughter and part frustration. "You know better than that." His hand came up, smoothing intimately over her soft belly and on up, cupping one breast in his callused hand. His thumb rasped over her nipple again and again, calling forth waves of shivering, pulsing sensation that tore through her in bursts of ever-increasing power. She gasped, her hips lifting, and the small movement shoved him even deeper within her.

And the floodgates burst. He began to move, his hands and mouth all over her, his hips flexing as he drove deep within her in great repeated strokes of power. His urgency swept her into the maelstrom and she began to move with him, urging him on with her hands and her body and hoarse exclamations of delight as the tension grew and stretched to an unbearable pitch. Her body was so sensitive that every motion was a sensual delight, every stroke and touch lighting small fires of passionate response within her. Above her, Cal gave a deep, incoherent cry and began to move in a forceful frenzied rhythm, his hips slamming into her with a raw power that quickly drove her to a wracking, shattering finish. But he didn't stop and her ecstasy went on and on, almost too much to bear, until he suddenly froze, his whole big body shuddering in her arms.

When the last tremors of reaction had faded and they lay silently, still joined in the darkness, Cal finally stirred. He rose from the bed and lifted her into his arms before she could even wonder what he was doing, then carried her into his room to the much larger bed.

"I can't sleep in there," he said in a husky voice, "So you'll sleep here from now on."

And with that settled, he flipped onto his back, drew her into his side as she'd been earlier in the day, and fell asleep.

She slept too, but she dreamed.

Someone was walking through the house. Hidden in the closet, she tried desperately to regulate her gasping breaths. A horrible thought occurred. She was bleeding from where he'd cut her. Had she left a trail to her hiding place?

But the feet walked past the closet and into the kitchen. Vivid curses, then a muffled thud and a groan.

"Where's my money, Galloway?"

Her ex-husband coughed. "I'm trying to get it together, I swear. I just need a few days—"

"That's what you said the last time."

"No, wait! I can get it. Just give me—"

A sullen thunk silenced the words. She'd never heard a silencer before but she knew, somehow, that she'd just heard the sound of a silenced bullet ending a life. Terror almost choked her.

The footsteps started again, walking out of the kitchen, and the killer paused right outside the closet door....

Her eyes flew open. Darkness. She knew immediately where she was, and she relaxed her rigid body, forcing herself to breathe slowly and deeply. Cal's arm tightened, drawing her to him, though she didn't think he was awake.

She cuddled closer, but her mind was racing. *She hadn't killed Wayne!*

Now the gold-plated question was; who had?

Seven

———

Lyn slipped out of the bed at dawn and tiptoed from the room.

Opening one eye, Cal watched her go, studying the long, elegant line of her back and the smooth globes of her bottom. She wasn't sneaking off, he knew, but going about her normal morning routine. When he got downstairs, there'd be fresh coffee and something hot ready to eat.

And this morning there would be a kiss, he thought with immense satisfaction.

He stretched, throwing back the covers and padding naked to the bathroom. She'd barely gotten out of the room yesterday before he realized what an ass he'd been. Still, it rankled that she might have given herself to him out of duty, so he'd dressed and taken the truck to town while he thought about the whole crazy thing.

He was attracted to Lyn. Amen, brother!

And she was attracted to him. He wasn't that stupid. She might have some dumb notion in her head about paying him back for his kindness, but she'd never have gone to bed with him if she didn't like his touch.

He splashed water over his face and reached for a towel, snatching at another of the worrisome thoughts running around in his head.

They hadn't used any protection. Unless she was on the pill, which he seriously doubted, they'd taken a big chance that could have consequences. *You took more than one.* He grinned at himself in the mirror. *Then the grin faded.*

He couldn't see the ending to this whole turn of events, and it worried him. He'd been wanting her for what seemed like forever. The problem was what happened when the sex stopped? He liked Lyn and would hate to see them part without salvaging their friendship, but he knew how women generally thought. He didn't know many men who still had friendships with the women in their affairs.

At the same time, he couldn't imagine life on the ranch without Lyn. She hadn't even been there a whole year and yet she'd left her stamp everywhere. There was hardly a thing she hadn't helped with, hardly a chore she wasn't willing to tackle. Fact was, she was a better rancher than he was half the time.

Yeah, but you can't expect her to devote the rest of her life to your ranch. Someday she's going to want a family of her own, instead of taking care of someone else's.

He didn't like *that* thought. Not at all. In fact, the idea of Lyn with someone else made him feel like kicking something. He paced the perimeter of the room with agitated strides, his brows drawn together.

It was only natural, he assured himself, since she'd slept with him, that he'd feel a little possessive.

So what are you going to do about it?

He shrugged on his shirt and started tucking it into his jeans. And suddenly, the answer was as clear as well water, right there staring him in the eye. *He would marry her.*

Marry her! It was a great idea. Practical as anything he'd ever done. He wanted a woman who liked the prairie, not a soft helpless flower like his mother had been. Lyn had been raised here. She knew all about the good and bad that came with ranching; she wouldn't just up and leave her husband and babies because she couldn't handle the hard work and the isolation.

And it neatly solved the other problem that had been gnawing at his mind since he woke. If Lyn was pregnant, marrying her would take care of that problem. Oh, he supposed he could wait and see if marriage was a necessity, but reality was that she was the kind of woman he'd been thinking of starting to look for. The fact that the sex was practically heart-stopping didn't really enter into it, he decided, although it certainly was a great bonus.

No question about it, she'd make a great wife. He nodded, feeling an inexplicable relief. Then, as he buckled his belt and reached for his boots, he began to ponder the next thought. Now, how did he convince Lyn? Her only experience with the institution of marriage had been less than ideal. She might not want to shackle herself to a man again.

He went down to breakfast full of purpose, determined to make her comfortable and happy so that she'd see how good their marriage could be. He'd take it slow and easy so she could get used to the idea of them as a couple. When he walked into the kitchen, she was pouring coffee into his mug at the table. She practically had him timed down to the second, a fact he appreciated.

"Morning." He walked across the room toward her.

"Good morning." Her cheeks grew pink as she turned away to set the coffeepot on its burner. He reached her before she could turn around again, sliding his hands around her waist and pulling her against him.

He bent his head and set his lips to the baby-soft skin just beneath her ear. "It's a *very* good morning," he said against her skin, aligning his body with hers.

She reached her hands behind her, stroking lightly up and down the backs of his thighs. "Uh-huh."

He raised one hand to her chin and tilted her face up and sideways so he could kiss her. She opened her mouth for him immediately and he took the offered treasure, stroking the inside of her mouth with his tongue, pulling her more tightly against him until she was clutching the backs of his thighs and they were both breathing hard.

He tore his mouth from hers. "How did I do without this kind of greeting before?"

She laughed, setting her hands over his and unfastening his grip on her. "I don't know. Do you want eggs or pancakes?"

He took her hand when she would have moved away. "Either. Both. Marry me, Lyn."

She stopped in mid-motion. Ever so slowly, she turned to face him and her eyes were huge pools of emerald in an incredulous face. "What did you say?"

He shrugged, watching her carefully, trying to gauge her reaction. Inside, he was cursing himself. Why had he blurted that out? Hadn't he just decided to go slowly? "I asked you to marry me."

She tugged her hand from his and hugged her arms around her body in a gesture that shouted defensiveness at him. "Cal, you don't marry someone because you've just had great sex with them."

He cursed himself for being impulsive. He kept his voice low, soothing. "I know. It's not that." Then he grinned. "Well, not just that," he said honestly. "Although that doesn't hurt." He moved to her again and placed his hands on her upper arms, lightly stroking up and down. "Don't give me an answer now. Let me explain what I've been thinking. Okay?"

She stared at him for a moment, her eyes shadowed and strangely vulnerable. A panicky fist began to squeeze his chest. What if she said no? At last, she nodded hesitantly. "All right. I'll listen." He dropped his hands and she stepped away. Then she turned back. "So which is it, eggs or pancakes?"

Over his bacon and eggs a few minutes later, he outlined for her all his reasons that a marriage between them made sense. They already knew they were compatible, both in bed and out. He wanted a woman who knew her way around a ranch, who loved the land. He needed a hard worker. His family knew and liked her....

"And there's one other thing."

Her eyebrows rose in enquiry.

"You might be pregnant. I didn't use protection. Any time."

She was blushing again, but she didn't refute his words. "I might be." She looked at him instead of twirling her spoon in her coffee as she'd been doing while he spoke, and her green eyes were direct. "You don't have to feel responsible for me, Cal, if that's what brought this on. I appreciate everything you've done for me but I can take care of myself now."

The panic that had begun to loosen its grip as he spoke rose so quickly it nearly choked him. "I *don't* feel responsible for you. Doesn't the fact that I've asked you to marry me without even knowing if I got you pregnant tell you that? Lyn, I'd like very much for you to be my wife. I'd like to make a life with you, work this ranch and have children with you, have wild sweaty sex with you." He leered suggestively, trying to lighten the atmosphere. "Would you like me to tell you more about that last one?"

She responded with a small, distracted smile as she rose. "I need to think about this, Cal. May I have a few days to consider?" Her face softened and she reached out and ran a single finger down the crease his dimple made in his cheek. "It's—it's a big step for me."

He understood. Marriage hadn't been a picnic for her the first time; her wariness was understandable. He turned his head and caught her finger in his mouth, swirling his tongue around the sensitive digit until her eyes clouded with pleasure, then he released it and pulled her into his lap. "I'm not like your ex-husband, baby. I respect your opinions and I hope you know I'd never mistreat you—"

"I know that, you silly man." Her husky voice was sweet. "It's just that…I need some time."

He sighed. He knew it wasn't unreasonable of her. But he wanted an answer today, dammit! He wanted to start making plans *right now*. "All right," he said grudgingly. "You can take some time to think."

He had a cow in the corral that he needed to take out to pasture, and he spent the rest of the day riding fence with one of his men while the others rode the other ends of the property. He figured once he had the place in shape he'd probably be able to work it with just two cowboys and occasional help from Lyn, but it was so run-down right now that he needed the extra workers.

Lyn had made a wonderful beef stew from the canned

beef she'd put up a few months ago and after dinner, he dragged her up the stairs to bed. They indulged in the wild sweaty sex he'd mentioned that morning and then he cuddled her in his arms as they lay watching the television in his bedroom for the weather reports and stock prices.

"If you're pregnant, will you marry me?" He lightly stroked her belly with one big hand.

Lyn heaved an exaggerated sigh. "You said you'd give me some time."

"I didn't say I wouldn't bug you about it, though." She chuckled.

"So, will you? If you're pregnant?"

She propped herself up on his chest, red curls floating over her shoulders and down around him, creating a curtain of intimacy. "I suppose I will, if it happens."

"Great!" He flipped her onto her back so fast she lay gasping beneath him. "Then all I have to do is get you pregnant."

"Cal! That's playing dirty," she complained. But her fingers were slipping between them, and he groaned when she found him, cupping him in her small hands, stroking the taut, growing flesh with sly fingers.

"I'll give you about two weeks to quit that," he said. He let her push him onto his back and she increased her ministrations, kneeling beside him at first, then swinging one long, slim white leg astride him. He touched her then, too, and they pleasured each other for long, unhurried minutes until shivers of back-arching pleasure began to race down his spine. Quickly, he grabbed her by the hips and dragged her down onto him just in time, and as he exploded within her, his upward thrusts urged her into her own finish and she threw her head back, her glorious hair streaming down her back, shaking as her body squeezed him repeatedly with rhythmic inner contractions.

When it was over, she fell forward to lie on his chest, limp and panting. He lifted a hand to stroke her hair.

"Yes," she whispered.

"Hmm?" He was too content to think, even.

"Yes, I'll marry you. If you're sure."

He ran both hands down her back and cupped the warm, smooth globes of her bottom. "Baby, I've never been more certain of anything in my life. We're going to be good together." Then he lifted his head and shot her a cocky grin. "And we're going to have a good marriage, too."

He took her to Rapid City for a marriage license the very next day, and when the clerk told them there was an opening in the justice's schedule, he took her by the hand. "Are you ready to do this?"

Lyn's eyes were as wide as they'd been when he'd first asked her to marry him yesterday. "I, ah, I guess so."

He shook his head at her. "Start practicing. The word is yes." Then he glanced at the clean but practical working clothes they both were wearing. "Will it bother you if we don't do this up the right way?"

She shook her head, and her shoulders sagged. "Not at all. It would be a huge relief."

"All right." He glanced at his watch. They had just enough time to get a ring if they didn't fool around. "We'll take the appointment," he told the clerk.

Fifteen minutes later, they walked into a jewelry store. Lyn lagged a step behind him, and he turned to cup her elbow. "Come on. I want you to see if there's anything you like here."

"You don't need to buy me a ring," she protested.

"I know. I *want* to buy you a ring." He looped an arm around her waist. He knew she hadn't grown up with much; now that she was his, he wanted to shower her with the best of everything.

She wouldn't make a decision about rings, though, and he finally asked the saleswoman to bring out several that he thought would look good on Lyn's long, elegant fingers. They were all lovely, but nothing in particular appealed to him, and Lyn had on her most serious poker face. If she liked one ring better than the rest, she wasn't about to tell him. The woman indicated another display. "I don't know if you've considered estate jewelry, but we have some gorgeous things. May I show them to you?"

Cal shrugged. "Sure."

The moment she returned, he saw the ring he liked, a stunning diamond set in a delicate filigree band with sizable rubies at each side. He pointed at the ring. "Let's see this one."

The moment she slipped on the ring, Lyn's face filled with wonder. "It's beautiful," she said reverently. Cal agreed. It was perfect. "Matches your hair," he murmured in her ear, smiling when she elbowed him. To the saleswoman, he said, "We'll take it." And when the woman suggested a simple ruby and diamond wedding band, he bought that, too, over Lyn's stunned protests.

The ring fit as if it had been made for her, and she wore it from the store. The wedding band he slipped into a pocket for the ceremony. Lyn hadn't suggested he wear a wedding band, and he congratulated himself again on making a good decision when he'd made up his mind to marry her. Some women would be upset about a man who wouldn't wear a ring, but Lyn understood without even discussing it that wedding rings and cowboys equaled missing fingers, often as not.

He saw a flower shop on the way to the courthouse and he left Lyn in the car while he ran in and had them quickly make up a bouquet of white roses and stargazer lilies. Lyn got tears in her eyes when he tossed them into her lap as he climbed into the truck, and he felt compelled to kiss them away, and one thing led to another until they were nearly late for their appointment.

Hand in hand they walked into the chamber where the justice awaited. The ceremony was brief and simple, but every word impressed itself into his mind. Lyn was somber and he wondered where her first wedding had been held. She had to be nervous about this. He squeezed her fingers and smiled at her reassuringly. The marriage was going to work well. How could it not?

Before they left Rapid, they stopped by the police station. He wanted to know if they'd learned anything more about who had shot Wayne Galloway. Detective Amick came hustling out of an office toward them when he asked about the investigation, narrowed eyes darting from Lyn to Cal to Lyn again. "What can we do for you today?" he asked.

"Just checking on how things are proceeding," Cal told him.

"Oh." He motioned them into the office, closing the door as his partner, Detective Biddle, stood and offered them his hand. "To tell you the truth, we've had absolutely no luck connecting anyone else to this crime." Amick's voice was flat and matter-of-fact. "We have a bullet but no weapon, no fingerprints or fibers and no witnesses." He cocked an eyebrow at Lyn. "Unless you want to share something new with us?"

Cal put a hand over Lyn's when she automatically began to talk. "We didn't come here so you could grill her, Detective."

"It's all right, I don't mind." Lyn clasped both hands on the table. "Actually, I've had a few flashes of what might be memories from that night."

All three men stared at her.

"Could you identify anyone?" asked Biddle, the older cop.

"No," she admitted. "But I know that this—" she touched the barely noticeable scar on her jaw "—was made by a pocketknife." She laid both hands flat on the desk before her. "Wayne came to me for money. Apparently he'd gotten into gambling or drugs—he didn't tell me what—but he had a big debt he couldn't pay. I didn't have any money and I wouldn't have given it to him if I had. He came after me and cut me with his pocketknife. I managed to shove him away and he hit his head and fell. He must have been knocked out. I hid. Wayne was in the kitchen. *Then someone else came in.*"

"Did you hear him speak?" Detective Biddle was sitting on the edge of his seat, scribbling on a notepad. "Get a look? Anything?"

She shook her head. "I did hear him speak but I didn't recognize the voice."

"And he's the one who shot Galloway?" Amick asked skeptically. "Why didn't he shoot you, too?"

"How did you get out of the closet and get away?" Biddle demanded.

Lyn spread her hands helplessly. "I don't know. But it's possible I'll remember something else. If I do, I'll call."

Back in the truck, Cal flexed his fingers on the steering wheel as the Black Hills receded behind them. "How long has it been since you started remembering?"

She shrugged. "I don't know. A couple of weeks."

"A couple of weeks," he repeated grimly. "And you didn't think it was important to tell me?"

"It *wasn't* important, really. I haven't remembered anything important."

"Lyn." He softened his voice with an effort. "It doesn't matter to me if there's another person in the picture. Your ex got what he deserved."

Her head whipped around. "What?"

"Just let it die," he said, trying to reassure her. "They told us they have next to nothing. Without a weapon they can't charge you."

Her mouth opened and closed; no sound came out. She looked down, toyed with the new rings she wore.

He got worried. "You okay?"

She nodded, still not looking at him. Finally, in a small voice, she said, "I can't believe we're really married."

He grinned. "I know. But it's real, baby. We'll get used to it together."

When they arrived at the ranch, the first thing Lyn did was go check on the gelding's hoof. Cal pulled on his old boots and was about to follow her when his eye lit on the telephone.

"You did *what* this morning?" His sister's shriek was loud enough to make him wince and yank the phone away from his ear.

"Got married," he repeated.

"To Lyn." Silver's voice sounded dazed. Then she rallied. "Well, I have to confess I was hoping you two might hit it off, but I can't believe you married her this morning." Her voice grew severe. "You rotten egg. I can't believe you didn't invite Mama and me."

"It was kind of sudden," he defended himself. "We

thought we'd get the license today but then they had a space in the schedule—''

"Excuses, excuses." His sister sighed. "It's going to take you a long time to earn back the points you've lost with this one, big brother."

He laughed. "Oh, man, I'm heartbroken. I really am."

"You can start making it up by bringing Lyn to dinner tonight. I'll have a little celebratory meal."

"A celebratory..." His good humor evaporated. He'd imagined having Lyn all to himself tonight. The last thing he wanted to do was spend the evening with his mother. "I don't know—"

"You have to have a special wedding supper," she argued. "Be here at six."

He should have known he wouldn't win that skirmish, he thought as he headed for the barn.

Later, Cal caught Lyn's horse by its bridle as she rode past him. "Where are you going?"

She stared patiently at him. "It's time to start dinner. Unless you'd rather."

He gave it a moment's thought. He'd been kicked in the ankle half an hour before by a wily cow who didn't intend to be corralled and he was still trying to wear the cussed thing down enough to round her up. "Maybe I should. But..."

"But what?"

"Silver invited us for dinner. So neither one of us has to cook."

She frowned. "Why did Silver invite us to dinner?"

He shrugged. "I told her we got married today. She insists on having a wedding supper."

"Oh, dear." Lyn's obvious consternation bothered him. She didn't seem the slightest bit pleased.

"Oh, dear, *what?*"

Her horse moved restlessly, and Cal realized he was still holding the bridle. He dropped his hand. "What are we going to tell them...I mean, won't they ask *why?*"

He suddenly realized what was bothering her, and his mood lightened immediately. "We'll tell them exactly what happened—Silver threw us together hoping to strike sparks, and it worked."

Silver threw us together hoping to strike sparks and it worked.

Lyn stepped out of the shower in her bathroom an hour later and reached for a towel, wrapping one around her dripping hair and drying her body with a second one. She walked into the bedroom and smoothed cream over her skin—with next to no humidity, skin dried out faster than a sheet on the line in a windstorm. And as she did, she thought about Cal's words. A reasonable enough explanation, she decided. And one that skirted the questions about love she hoped no one would ask.

Her engagement ring flashed in the light as she pulled on panties, and she stopped to admire it again. This still felt like a dream. Cal married to her? She'd wished for many things since she'd come to live with him but this...this was truly beyond her wildest imaginings.

Her dream scampered ahead a few years, and she automatically put a hand over her abdomen. Children. She couldn't imagine herself pregnant with Cal's child but she could see Cal on his horse with two or three young boys trailing behind him. The image made her smile. Of course, they could all be daughters—which didn't preclude them from riding with their father.

Their father. And she would be their mother. No, she couldn't imagine it. A family of her own. She'd stopped dreaming after Wayne. The closest she'd come since was at the wedding ceremony this morning, when they'd been speaking their vows. Cal had pledged to take her forever for his wife, and for just a second, she'd wished love was a part of what they shared. *His* love for her. But then common sense had inserted itself into her longing and she'd reminded herself to be grateful. She loved Cal, and she'd never thought she'd have this much. To be married to him, about to start a life that she prayed would last until they were ages old...yes, she'd be happy with what she had.

She'd make herself be.

But as she stepped into her jeans and buttoned her blouse, she remembered his words in the truck on the way home from town. She'd been so shocked and stunned she hadn't been able to answer him when she realized he didn't believe her. He didn't believe there had been someone else in her apartment the day Wayne died.

Which meant he believed she had killed her husband.

The thought was almost enough to bring tears to her eyes, but she concentrated on forcing them back. With as little evidence as there was, she guessed she couldn't blame him. And God knew, if she'd had the chance to kill Wayne during some of the years he'd knocked her around, she might have tried it.

But it hurt, *a lot,* that Cal had thought she was lying. It reminded her forcefully that this marriage wasn't an ordinary one, that she could never expect the emotional support other women in loving relationships could expect. If Cal loved her, he'd never have suspected her of lying.

His voice bellowed up the stairs then, interrupting her thoughts. "Lyn? Are you about ready?"

Just as well, she decided, heading down to join him. She intended to take as much happiness from this marriage as she could. There was no sense dwelling on what wasn't to be; she'd be grateful for what was.

Silver had done as much as she could in one afternoon. White paper wedding bells hung above the table and there was a centerpiece—a beautiful arrangement of white flowers with five candles rising from it. Real cloth napkins and a tablecloth, the lovely china and crystal she and Deck had received from Cora Lee as wedding gifts, and on the sideboard, a two-layer cake smothered in white icing with a tiny bride and groom in a circle of flowers adorning the top.

Everyone kissed and congratulated Lyn. To her shock and delight, Silver had called Rilla Weston from the women's shelter, and Rilla had driven all the way from Rapid to be there for dinner. Cal's mother hugged her close, whispering, "I couldn't have chosen a better daughter-in-law myself. Welcome to the family, dear."

Lyn cried. She couldn't help it. This family had treated her with a kindness she'd rarely known in her life, and now she would be one of them. It was too much.

"Now, now," said Silver, putting an arm around her and hugging her. "I know marrying my brother is real hardship."

Cal bared his teeth at her as Lyn smiled through the tears. He reached out and plucked Lyn from Silver's embrace, wrapping his arms around her and pressing her face into his shoulder. "Marrying your brother is her good fortune," he informed Silver. He leaned back and looked down at Lyn, holding her gaze with his own. "And marrying her is mine."

Lyn's breath caught in her throat at the look in his eye. Then it hit her—he was putting on a show for his mother and sister. That warm light gleaming in his eye was for their benefit. Straightening, she gently pulled herself out of his arms and turned to Silver again.

"Thank you," she said. "How on earth did you accomplish all this in one afternoon?"

"We got the flowers and bells at the flower shop in Kadoka," Cora Lee said. "And Rilla, bless her heart, brought the figurines. We made the cake ourselves."

"And you did a fine job," Rilla assured her.

"We were going to try for a three- or four-tier look but we knew our limits." Silver's eyes danced.

Rilla had a camera hanging by a strap around her neck, and she began snapping photos. "We have to have some mementos of this day," she said happily.

Cora Lee clapped her hands. "What a wonderful thought. I completely forgot about pictures."

Deck had been standing in the doorway when they arrived. He strode across the room and swept Lyn into a crushing hug, then offered his hand to Cal. "Congratulations. This is the smartest thing you've ever done, old buddy."

"Possibly." Cal returned the handshake, then admitted, "Probably."

Deck grinned. "Come on in the den. These women have been cooking like fools all afternoon. I figure we're best off to stay out of the way."

Silver caught Lyn's hand. "And *you*—come with us. I want to know why I didn't have a clue that my brother was romancing you."

"It wasn't exactly like that," Lyn protested.

Cal stopped in the doorway of the den and looked back at her. "It *was* exactly like that," he corrected. He grinned at his sister. "Don't tell me you weren't doing a little matchmaking when you asked me to hire her."

"Well," Silver admitted. "The thought might have

crossed my mind. But I wasn't sure you were bright enough to see what a gem you have here.''

"Oh, I saw," said Cal softly, returning his gaze to Lyn. "I definitely saw."

As her new sister-in-law and mother-in-law pulled Lyn into the kitchen, Lyn closed her eyes briefly to regroup. Cal couldn't have made it plainer that he expected her to play the role of loving bride in front of his family.

"Oh, my word." Silver had caught Lyn's left hand and now she held it up to examine her rings. "Look at this, Mama!"

"It's absolutely stunning, dear." Cal's mother eyed the ring with what Lyn suspected was expert knowledge. "You have a good eye."

"Oh, I didn't pick it out," Lyn said hastily. "Cal chose this one." Then, lest they think she didn't like it, she added, "Although it's the most beautiful ring I've ever seen. I loved it the moment I saw it."

Cora Lee had a faraway look in her eyes. "My son has excellent taste."

"He got it from you, Mama." Silver laid a gentle hand on her mother's shoulder.

But Cora Lee shook her head slowly. "Cal didn't spend enough time with me during his childhood to get *anything* from me."

Lyn squeezed her hand, sensing a deep melancholy beneath the words. "He's gentle and thoughtful and kind, just like you and Silver. It runs in the family."

Eight

Cal eyed Lyn across the table as he and Deck finished the last two pieces of the wedding cake. She'd been quiet all evening. Not really unusual in itself—Lyn was always a quiet presence. And with three other women all gabbing at once, she'd barely opened her mouth. But he sensed something was bothering her.

His bride was talking with his mother, unaware that he watched her. Her red hair was caught back in a loose French braid, and curly wisps had escaped to form a burnished halo around her head. Her green eyes danced as she and Rilla laughed at something his mother had said, and her soft cheeks were flushed with pink.

He remembered the pink and white perfection of her long, slender frame and his body tightened. Her skin was so milky white it was translucent, especially the fragile flesh at her wrists and behind her knees, and over her breasts, where a delicate tracery of fine blue veins showed through. Her nipples were a pale pink, their centers just a shade darker—until he suckled her, and then they flushed a rosy hue that turned him on even more. He shifted in his seat, and from across the table, Deck sent him a knowing look.

"Ready to leave, are you?"

Cal knew his smile was wry. "You bet." He looked at Lyn. "It's been a big day. Are you ready to go?"

She gazed at him and from the way she blushed he suspected she'd read every thought in his lecherous mind. "Yes, I'm ready," she said quietly.

He made their farewells brief because she really did look exhausted and he hustled her out to the truck. The drive home took only ten minutes, and he lifted her into his arms when she stepped down from the truck, carrying her inside and up to their bed despite her protests.

"You're a feather," he told her. "I could carry you if you weighed twice this much."

"When I'm pregnant, I just might," she said darkly.

He laughed. Moments later, he slid naked into the bed, sighing with relief when he pulled her soft, bare curves against him. He needed her desperately and he showed her so, kissing her with deep intent, stroking her pretty body repeatedly, seeking out all the tender spots he was beginning to learn were her most sensitive. At first, she was passive in his arms, and he wondered if she was too tired for lovemaking. But then she began to respond, her slim arms winding around his neck, her long, muscled legs wrapping around him to hold him to her.

Her response aroused him further, and he shoved his hips against her while he slipped one big hand over her bottom to explore the warm crease. She arched against him, and his fingers slipped into the hidden valley between her legs. He probed with one finger, sliding a little way into her, making her shudder and arch against him again. He pressed harder, his finger sliding even farther into her hot, sweet channel. He was fully erect, pushing at her belly, and when she wriggled against his invading finger, she stroked him with her soft curls, encouraging his possession. Someday, he promised himself, someday he'd take this slow and easy, but not right now....

Rigid, needy, he withdrew his hand and reared back to position himself, then plunged into her with a single heavy stroke that carried him deep, deep inside her. Her legs climbed his back, and he fell into a heavy, beating rhythm that rocked her body with the force of his thrusts. She whimpered, and he caught the sound with his mouth.

"Okay?" he whispered against her mouth.

"No. No, I want...I want...."

He covered her mouth with his again, drinking deep, glorying in her response. "Sh, baby, I've got what you want." He worked his hand between their bodies until he could feel his flesh plunging and withdrawing from her as he teased out the fleshy nubbin at the top of her sweet opening. Gently, he took her between his fingers, squeezing and releasing the tender flesh. She screamed into his chest, and he felt a sudden sharp shock of sweet pain as her teeth fastened on his shoulder. Tremors shook her, and then the soft squeeze of her internal contractions milked his length. A groan tore from his throat; it felt too good...too good...and he let go of what little control he had left, pounding into her for a few frantic seconds until his body stiffened and he reached his own climax, his arching back pushing him deep within her to deliver his seed.

A few minutes later, when he'd gotten his breath back, he leaned his forehead against hers. "We need to talk about babies."

Her eyes were closed and a soft smile played over her lips. She nodded.

He couldn't resist; he reached down and pinched her bottom.

Her eyes flew open. "Ouch! What was *that* for?"

"Just making sure you're awake."

"I'm awake. I was just…recovering."

He chuckled. "Yeah. Me, too."

Then her beautiful eyes found his in the dim light of the single lamp he'd switched on. "We didn't use anything. Again."

"I know. We could have hit the lottery already." He hesitated. "If you're pregnant, I'll be thrilled. But if you're not…I think I'd like to wait a little while before adding to our family."

She didn't speak, but her eyes held questions.

He dropped his head and kissed her slowly, lingering over her response. "I'd like us to have a little time together first."

A flare of surprise lit her eyes before she nodded. "I'd like that, too."

"Or," he said, "maybe I'm just selfish. I want this body to myself for a while before I have to share." He moved from her then, settling himself and pulling her into his arms. She'd slept draped across his chest last night and he'd liked it. He'd liked it a lot. She'd be sleeping like that every night from now on.

She woke him in the middle of the night, moaning and thrashing around.

He laid her back and leaned over her, wondering if he should wake her. Then her eyes opened wide, and she screamed.

It scared the hell out of him and he jerked backward

in surprise. Then he realized she was still asleep. Her
eyes had slowly drifted closed again and the tight fists of
her hands loosened. Her legs stopped their restless movements and she sighed. Then a single tear fell from the
corner of her eye. He couldn't stand the sight of her crying, and he gathered her into his arms, willing away her
distress. He hadn't known whether to believe her or not
when she'd told the detectives she was beginning to remember the day of the murder. But the more he thought
about it, he knew Lyn had too much integrity to lie, even
if the lie might mean the difference between jail and free-
dom.

As he rocked her gently against his chest, she seemed
to relax into a normal sleep. He closed his arms securely
around her, and as he drifted to sleep, he made a mental
note to ask her in the morning if she remembered having
a bad dream. If her subconscious had revealed anything
else about the man who'd murdered her ex-husband, then
he wanted to know about it.

Cal reached out and slapped his hand over the alarm
button, and the room suddenly went silent again. Lyn lay
where she'd slept for a minute, loving the solid sheet of
muscle beneath her cheek, the beat of his heart in her
ear, the strength in the arm that clasped her to him. She
hated to move, but life on a ranch didn't wait for late
sleepers.

Slowly, she began to slide away, but Cal's arm tightened. "Don't get up," he growled.

She smiled against his chest. "Not an option."

He was silent. Finally, he said, "Dammit, you're
right," in a grumpy tone that made her laugh aloud as
she walked into the bathroom.

She was downstairs making the coffee when she remembered the dream. She'd been in the closet of her apartment in Rapid City again, her heart pounding so loud she thought the man who'd just walked through the hallway could hear her.

"Where's the woman?" It was a stranger's voice, muttering as if to himself.

Wayne didn't answer. She thought she knew why. He was dead, shot by the person walking through her home.

The footsteps moved farther from her hiding place, back the hall toward the bedroom. She could hear the man whistling—whistling!—under his breath.

The bathroom door at the very end of the hall creaked open, and she knew that if she was going to get out, she had to go now while she had as great a lead as possible. Silently, praying that the door hadn't developed a creak, she pushed it ajar just far enough to slip through. Her keys were on the hook right beside the door, thank God, and she clutched them in her fist as she eased open the front door.

"Hey!" It was a rough masculine voice, and she jumped a foot in the air. Automatically she slammed the door behind her. No sense in worrying about noise now. Maybe it would slow him down a little. Her old truck, all she'd been able to afford after the divorce, was parked right in front of the apartment, and she sprinted down the steps, missing half of them and nearly breaking her neck. She could hear her pursuer shouting as she wrenched open the door and jammed the key into the ignition and then the sound of his shoes slapping the sidewalk as he ran. Her breath was coming in hitches, sobs of pure terror forcing themselves out of her throat.

She pushed the truck into reverse—

And suddenly a hand slapped against the glass of the driver's side window. She screamed and pushed the gas

*pedal hard and the truck shot backward all the way out
of the parking lot and onto the street. Shoving at the
gearshift again, she managed to get it into drive and
slammed her foot onto the pedal again, squealing down
the street and out of the neighborhood like a teenager in
a souped-up hot rod.*

And that was it. All she remembered. She'd never seen
the face of the man who'd murdered Wayne and surely
would have killed her. She still didn't know why she'd
driven all the way to her old home, and she might never.

And the detectives from Rapid City would continue to
believe she'd killed her ex-husband.

And so would Cal.

That thought was too hurtful to acknowledge, so she
ignored it. She wondered why the detectives were so reluctant to believe her. She supposed it was their duty to
consider her a suspect until she had an ironclad alibi, and
she was certain they'd already have slammed her into a
jail cell if not for Cal's intervention. Their attitudes made
Joe Parker, the local sheriff, seem sweet.

Cal came in, and she handed him the coffee she'd just
poured, then finished the French toast she'd been frying,
sliding the last pieces on a plate and retrieving the syrup
from the microwave where she'd heated it. She took her
seat at the table at the same time Cal did.

As he transferred several pieces of bacon to his plate,
he asked, "Do you remember having any dreams last
night?"

His voice was too casual, and immediately her mental
defenses went up. What had she said or done in her
sleep? Carefully, she kept her eyes on her plate as she
shrugged. "Not really. Why?" Cal hadn't believed her
when she'd told him someone else was involved in
Wayne's murder, and she couldn't forget that.

He shrugged, too, but he was watching her closely. "No special reason. You were a little restless." Then his face relaxed and he grinned. "This time yesterday," he said in a thoughtful voice, "we weren't married yet."

She smiled, pleased that he seemed to have accepted her answer. "This time yesterday we weren't planning on getting married yesterday!"

He grinned. "Yeah, but I'm glad we did." He reached for her hand, rubbing his thumb over the rings he'd given her. "This is a pretty comfortable arrangement, isn't it?"

Comfortable. She managed a nod, though there was an ache in her heart that nearly took her breath. She didn't *want* to be comfortable, darn it! She wanted to be loved.

When she realized what she'd just admitted to herself, she spoke unthinkingly. "Oh, boy."

"What?" He looked at her curiously.

"Nothing," she said hastily. She withdrew her hand from his and picked up her fork. *Idiot!* she berated herself. *Why can't you be happy with what you have?* She didn't know the answer to that. She could survive with what she and Cal had between them, she knew, because she'd survived far worse. And she could even be reasonably happy this way, living with and loving the man. But she didn't want to be reasonably happy. She wanted to be deliriously, ridiculously ecstatic about her marriage and her husband.

Other women had it; why shouldn't she? She glanced at Cal as he cut his French toast into squares, his eyes far away. He was thinking about the day's work, she knew. If only he were thinking of her. He cared about her, she was sure. And he was attracted to her, of that she also was sure. Could those things mature into love?

Hope bloomed within her as they finished the meal,

and when he looked up and caught her eyes on him, she gave him a blinding smile.

He stared for a second, then his eyes narrowed in the way she was growing to know so well.

"Oh, no, you don't," she said, scrambling to her feet and starting toward the sink with her dishes. "We have to brand those last few calves this morning, remember?"

He came up behind her with his own dishes, setting them on the counter and trapping her with his body. He was hard and already aroused, and she felt her insides turn to jelly as he dropped his head and nuzzled at her ear. "There are only three," he said. "We have time."

She turned to face him, allowing her hands to slip between them and start to work on his belt buckle. "You're right. Besides, we're newlyweds."

His surprise showed in his eyes, but he was quick to take her up on her ready acceptance. "We'll have to think of another excuse when that one gets old," he informed her as his mouth came down on hers.

The calves were branded, castrated and vaccinated a little later than Cal had planned that morning. But if any of the hands wondered why the boss was running late, nobody was brave enough to ask.

The next several days were quiet and routine. A couple of bulls went missing and had to be brought home, the calves they were weaning began to eat cake, a buffalo from the neighboring outfit knocked down a pile of McCall fences on a morning stroll. Lyn loved the outdoor work, especially anything that gave her a chance to ride. But she made sure she didn't neglect the inside of the house. Cal had hired her to keep his house clean and feed him well, and she wasn't going to change that now that they were married.

She defrosted a big pumpkin and used it to make two pies and loaves of pumpkin bread, cooked off a chicken and made a big pot of chicken noodle soup and put together two beef casseroles, which she froze for branding time or a busy day, whichever came first.

The next afternoon, she called Cal's mother and invited her to dinner again.

"Why, thank you, dear. That would be lovely. I have to leave the day after next." Cora Lee hesitated. "Does Cal know you called?"

Lyn cleared her throat, suddenly uncomfortable. "Not specifically, no, but I know he'll be delighted."

His mother's laugh was genuine. "You and I both know that's a fib, Lyn McCall." Her voice grew firm and serious. "But I'm coming anyway. I intend to be a part of your lives whether he likes it or not. His children aren't going to grow up without knowing I love them."

Lyn had a lump in her throat. She wondered again what had happened between Cal's parents. Cora Lee hadn't wanted to leave her son behind, Lyn was certain, despite what Cal thought.

When he came in to wash up, she told him his mother was coming over for dinner. "She's what? Let me guess. She called and invited herself again." Cal so rarely spoke sarcastically that Lyn's gaze flew to his face. Her hands stilled over the pumpkin bread she was slicing.

"No," she said slowly. "I called her. She leaves in two days and I thought you'd like—"

"You thought wrong." His voice was cold. "That woman left my father and me without a backward glance. Then when her nice, neat *socially acceptable* little world was stable again she remembered me. It's a little late for a devoted mother act."

Lyn bowed her head. The fragile sense of contentment

she'd been feeling for the past several days shriveled and died. "I'm sorry. Shall I call and cancel?"

There was a tense silence in the kitchen. Finally, Cal heaved a sigh. "No. No, don't cancel it. I suppose I can endure one more meal with my mother before she sails away again, never to return."

"But—" Lyn's head came up. "Cal, she's coming back when Silver's baby is born. And she'll come on a regular basis to see her grandchildren, I'm sure. When our children are born—"

"When our children are born that woman's not staying here." His voice was adamant. "And I wouldn't hold my breath waiting for her to come back and visit. You'll die of lack of oxygen."

Lyn didn't see that there was anything she could say that wouldn't infuriate Cal, so she chose silence as a better course of action. Cal stomped up the steps to shower and change, and she finished slicing the bread with shaking hands.

He was done in the shower by the time she went upstairs to take her own shower. After she was done, she began getting the meal organized. He came out of the office a few minutes later and snatched his hat off the peg, then took down the truck keys. "I'll be back with your guest in a few minutes," he said, not even looking at her before he went out the back door.

Lyn's heart sank. Was he going to be this difficult all evening? It would certainly be an awkward meal if he was. She ached for him. Beneath the cold facade with which he dealt with his mother was a little boy who still wondered why she'd left him behind. Cal was normally the kindest of men; only an emotional reaction this strong would make him behave this way.

True to his word, he was back in a few minutes, and

as Lyn welcomed Cora Lee into the house, she was relieved to note that he once again wore the cool but affable face he usually presented to his mother.

"It's cold out there," he said as he helped her out of her coat. "We'll have to chop ice again tomorrow morning."

"Cal was telling me that you helped with the branding," his mother said, rubbing her hands together to warm them. She shook her head. "I admire you, dear."

"Lyn's tough. She'll make a good ranch wife." Cal's voice was expressionless, but the color drained from Cora Lee's face. She bit her lip as the implied criticism hung in the air.

Frowning at Cal, Lyn thrust a bowl of vegetables into his hands. "Here. Set these on the table, please." She put an arm around his mother's shoulders and guided her to a seat. "I was born and raised here," she said. "Actually, I wasn't raised so much as I was dragged up. My mother died when I was young, and my father didn't know what to do with a little girl."

Cora Lee smiled. "He did a fine job."

Thankfully, Lyn was saved from responding to that when Cal took his seat and began to pass the dishes. The meal went better than she'd expected, though she talked more than normal and she was very aware of the prolonged silences that fell when she stopped directing the conversation.

Cora Lee watched Cal with a hungry intensity that was painful for Lyn to see. She appeared almost to be memorizing everything she could about him.

Cal, in turn, either didn't see his mother's scrutiny or chose to ignore it. Lyn wasn't certain which it was. When he'd scarfed down his second piece of pie and the meal ended, Cal rose from the table and stood with one big hand on the back of his chair.

"You'll have to excuse me, ladies. I have some office work that can't wait." He looked across the table at his mother, and his eyes were as cool and hard as granite. "I'll be happy to take you back to Silver's whenever you like." Then he turned and left the room.

A heavy silence filled the void he left.

Finally, Cora Lee said, "Well, I wouldn't want to interfere with his routine. I'm sure he's terribly busy getting this place to rights again." Her soft Southern drawl was more slurred than usual, and Lyn realized the older woman was fighting tears.

"He's not *that* busy," she said sharply. "He's being terribly rude. Can I apologize for him?"

His mother shook her head. "No need." She sighed and ran a gentle finger around the rim of her glass. "I understand how hurt he must have been as a little boy. I just—" She stopped, her breath hitching. Lyn twisted her fingers together in painful knots as she watched Cora Lee win the battle for self-control. "I'm sorry, dear. Perhaps you could just run me back and then I wouldn't have to bother Cal."

"Mrs. Jenssen, Cora Lee…" Lyn hesitated. "Have you ever tried to talk to Cal? Explain your side of the story?"

The woman nodded sadly. "He won't listen. You've seen the way he keeps me at a polite distance."

Lyn had. It drove her crazy. As she'd said to him once, he was lucky that he had a mother at all. And his mother seemed to love him dearly, despite whatever misunderstanding stood between them. Didn't he have any notion how precious that was? She hesitated again. She wasn't a person to interfere, but if Cora Lee didn't tell her about her years on the plains, Lyn might never know. If she had children someday, she'd like them to have a balanced picture. "How did you meet his father?"

Cora Lee smiled the tiniest bit. "I was on vacation with my family. We had toured the Badlands and decided to go to a local rodeo right here in Kadoka. Tom was a contestant in the bronc riding." She sighed, her eyes going cloudy as she looked back in time. "Honey, I thought he was just about the best-looking man I'd ever come across."

"Does Cal look like him?"

"Yes." She linked her fingers and set her hands precisely in her lap, ever the lady. "Yes, he does. Tom was big and dark-haired—the only difference was that he had beautiful blue eyes."

And Cal had inherited his mother's.

"Once he batted those eyes at me, I was hooked," she said, chuckling. "I thought I couldn't live without him. We ran off to Rapid City the next day and got married."

Lyn gasped. "The next *day?*"

Cora Lee nodded. "Can you believe it?"

"What on earth did your parents say?"

"They weren't pleased. But I was eighteen and headstrong and in love with the sexiest cowboy God ever made and I wasn't sorry. Not even when my daddy said he'd disinherit me." She looked down at her hands. "No, I wasn't sorry then."

There was another silence in the kitchen. Lyn caught Cora Lee's eye. Softly, she said, "What happened?"

The other woman sighed. "Tom was nine years older than I was. He already had this place, but it was pretty rough then. He brought me back here to live and…"

"And you quickly learned that a cowboy works from

sunup to sundown and expects his wife to do the same thing.''

"It wasn't only that," Cal's mother said in her soft Southern drawl. "I didn't mind the cooking and the cleaning. But I never saw Tom except at night." To Lyn's amazement, she blushed. "Those nights surely were fine, but little by little, the isolation got to me. I hardly ever saw other women because Tom was just starting his outfit and we weren't wealthy." She shrugged. "We only had the one truck so I rarely got to town and when I did, the local ladies all knew each other and I was a stranger from the East. And I started missing the mountains at home, and trees. It's so *barren* out here.''

Lyn nodded. "I grew up loving this land, but it isn't easy. And on a blazing summer day when the dust chokes you, you have to love it to put up with it." She smiled. "I think I'd get claustrophobic living where there are trees and mountains blocking your view. I'm not even real fond of the Black Hills!''

"So you can understand how I felt about the place I was raised.''

"Yes, I think I can.''

"Well, I got pregnant almost right away. I was terribly sick during much of my pregnancy so I was even more isolated—I can remember just crying and crying for home, my mother, *anything* familiar.''

"You were practically a child," Lyn said indignantly. "Your husband should have been a little more attentive to your feelings.''

Cora Lee smiled wryly. "It wasn't all Tom's fault. The poor man didn't have a clue how to handle a tearful teenager. And then Cal was born less than a year after we got married." Her face lit up. "He was the most beautiful little boy. I adored him. And I loved being a mama. But by then, things weren't so good between Tom and me. He thought I was stuck-up for not wanting to be around the other women. I wasn't," she said indignantly, "I was *shy*. And I still couldn't get used to the prairie. I hated the snow that was so deep we were stuck here for days. It broke my heart when Tom found calves frozen to death. I watched the horizon constantly in the summer for tornadoes. My flowers died. Hail killed my vegetables." She snorted. "I wasn't used to growing my own, anyway, and the hail just added insult to injury...." She trailed off. "I was a pathetic excuse for a wife. In Tom's eyes, anyway. I think he was sorry he married me."

Into the silence, Lyn said, "I'm sure he loved you."

Cora Lee shrugged. "He was attracted to me. I'm not sure about the love." She rose and began to stack dishes as if she couldn't bear to be still any longer. "When Cal was almost a year old, I'd had enough. I couldn't take one more day out here, much less a second winter. I called my daddy and he said I should come home."

"So you left," Lyn said softly. She rose, too, and walked to the sink to start some dishwater.

"Yes." She exhaled heavily, leaning both hands on the counter. "I wanted to take Cal with me. But Tom wouldn't hear of it. We had some terrible fights. Finally, he told me that if I took his son, he'd come after him. He said he'd tell everyone at home how I'd run off...he said he'd tell them I'd been with other men and wasn't a fit mother...." She whirled and faced Lyn. "I know this might seem stupid to you, but I was raised in a wealthy Southern family where scandal simply is not tolerated. Even a hint of something improper sticks like glue. If it had only been me, I wouldn't have cared. But it would have affected Mama and Daddy, our whole family." Her voice was bitter. "Southerners *of good family,*" she said in a mocking voice, "can be a cruel, insular group. It might have been the twentieth century, but there were still some mighty rigid standards in place."

Lyn didn't know how to respond. What Cora Lee was describing was so far outside her admittedly limited experience that it hardly seemed credible. Still...*she* believed it, and that was what was important. "So you left Cal with his father."

"Not exactly." The older woman sat heavily on one of the bar stools. "I couldn't leave without my son. I told Tom I wouldn't go then, but he threw me out. Bought me a plane ticket back to Virginia and told me I'd never get through the front door of his home again." She looked around her former husband's home with a rueful half smile. "He's probably rolling over in his grave right about now!"

"He *should* be. Tyrant." Lyn was so shocked she could barely speak.

"I cried for weeks. Months." Her eyes were misting, and Lyn could feel her own tears welling up. "I called but Tom would hang up. Daddy contacted a lawyer in Rapid City who laughed and said there was no way I could get Cal since I'd abandoned him." She put her hands to her eyes and pressed fiercely. "Eventually my divorce was final, and a couple of years after that I met Silver's daddy."

"But...your—Tom allowed Cal to begin visiting with you?"

Cora Lee nodded behind her hands. "When Cal got old enough to start asking hard questions, Tom relented a little. He let me have Cal for a week or two every summer." She took her hands away from her face and the tears rolled down her cheeks. "You can't imagine— I *lived* for those few days every year. But every year Cal grew a little more distant. Even when he came that summer after the accident he wouldn't let me comfort him—''

"Ready to leave, Mother?" It was Cal's voice, deep and mocking.

Both women jumped. Lyn's gaze flew to the archway to the living room, where he'd apparently come out of his office…when? Cal's jaw was clenched, his face a stony mask. But his eyes were alive, livid and leaping with fury.

"Cal." Instinctively she reached out a hand. "What— how—''

"How much did I hear?" He sneered, and the expression was so ugly he didn't even look like her husband. "The whole touching tale.''

"I'll get my coat." Cora Lee's face was as white as the hand soap at the sink.

"I'll take her home." Lyn started to walk toward the mudroom where the coats were but Cal stepped forward and caught her by the arm.

"I'll do it."

Lyn went still. She'd sworn to herself that she would never allow any man to touch her in anger again. "Take your hand off me," she said in a low, flat voice.

To his credit, he released her instantly. "I wasn't going to hurt you."

She turned her back on him. "Give me the keys."

"No. She's my—''

"I said give me the keys!"

She didn't know which one of them was more shocked. Cal's head snapped back as if she'd struck him.

She clapped a hand over her mouth.

They stared at each other through a space far more vast than the few feet separating them across the kitchen.

Then the same blank expression slipped over his features again. Silently, he reached into his pocket and withdrew the keys, tossing them to her.

The jarring jangle of the keys was the only sound as she turned, equally silently, and walked into the mud-room. Cora Lee stood in a small, miserable hunch at the door. When Lyn got her coat on, she opened the door and gestured for Cal's mother to precede her.

He was still standing where she'd left him. She started to walk out the door, then stopped, though she didn't turn to face him. Quietly, she said, "Shall I come back?"

There was total silence behind her for a moment and she thought he might say no. Her heart skipped a beat. Then he spoke in a deep, toneless voice. "I'm not my father. I won't throw you out of your home."

Nine

He was watching the news when she got back.

How should she handle this? Instinct told her Cal wouldn't bring it up. The man was a master at sweeping undesirable emotions under the rug. The same instinct told her, though, that if the wounds his little-boy's heart had suffered were ever to heal cleanly, they had to talk about what his mother had revealed.

It was an unfair position for Fate to place her in. She loved Cal too much to see him suffer for the rest of his life. On the other hand, she could lose whatever chance she had of winning his love if she forced him to confront his past. Neither choice, she thought bleakly, was palatable.

She finished cleaning up the kitchen and then joined him in the living room. Since the first time they'd made love, he'd begun sitting on the couch with her cuddled in his arm while they checked the news and weather. But tonight he was back in the recliner where he'd sat before.

Her heart sank, but she quietly took her usual seat on the couch and opened the basket that contained her sewing. She had a button to sew onto one of Cal's shirts, and when she had finished that, she resumed work on the tiny sweater set she was knitting for Deck and Silver's baby. She was finished with the sweater itself and nearly done the hat, and she was sure she'd have the dainty booties done before Christmas.

The room was silent except for the drone of the newscaster. How to begin?

"If you heard the whole story," she said, as if they'd been in the middle of a rational discussion, "then you know your mother didn't just walk away and forget you."

He turned his head and looked at her, and his eyes were a frozen lake of gray. "She can twist the story any way she likes. My father can't defend himself anymore."

"Your father told you your mother was an aristocratic snob, true?"

"Your point being?"

"Think about it," she said forcefully. "For such a terrible snob, she surely seemed friendly with Rilla. God knows Rilla will never win any prizes for gentility, but she's got a big heart. She's also a good judge of people and she liked your mother."

He didn't answer, merely compressed his lips into an even grimmer line.

"You heard her explain why she never made friends here," she said desperately. "And anyone could see that her heart still aches at the memory of leaving you—"

"No!" He slammed a fist down on the arm of his chair, and she jumped. "I married you because I wanted

a steady, sensible wife who could handle ranch living."
His eyes weren't cold any longer, but hot and turbulent.
"I *didn't* ask you to butt into my personal life."

Every word sliced into her tender heart like butcher
knives. *A steady, sensible wife...* Every dream she'd ever
had of Cal returning her love shriveled into dust and blew
away like prairie topsoil. Slowly, she bowed her head and
stared at the floor so he wouldn't see the trembling lip
she was biting so fiercely. "No. You didn't."

"Then don't try to change me," he said. "Either take
me and this marriage the way you found them or..." He
didn't finish the sentence but the implication ricocheted
around the room as if he'd shouted it.

She could hardly see her needlework for the tears that
flooded her eyes, but she kept her gaze on it anyway. She
couldn't have looked at him if she'd been ordered to. It
was too painful to view the death of all the hopes she'd
had for the future.

Cal got to his feet. He crossed to the door, and as he
passed her, he hesitated for a moment. But she kept her
head down, willing herself to concentrate on making her
shaking fingers complete the tiny purls on which she was
working, and after a long, tense couple of heartbeats, he
walked out of the room and up the stairs.

And her fingers stilled as the tears fell.

After what seemed like a long time but probably was
less than an hour, she stirred. The forgotten needlework
lay in her lap, and she folded it carefully and put it away.
Then she rose, slowly, feeling like a creaky old woman,
and went methodically through the house turning off
lights. At the top of the stairs, she paused. Did Cal expect
her to sleep with him tonight?

The door to the room she'd been coming to think of
as theirs was slightly ajar, the way it usually was at night.

But she couldn't bring herself to walk into that room and slide into bed with him. He'd made it very clear that while he might want her body, he certainly didn't want or need any of her emotions in his marriage. *A steady, sensible wife...*

So she slipped into her old room and got ready for bed, then turned out the last light after she'd climbed in and pulled up the covers.

At the other end of the hall, Cal lay alone in the bed he'd shared with his wife for the past several nights. Though there was little light, he stared, eyes dry and burning, at the ceiling. He'd heard her go into her old room and realized that she wasn't planning to sleep with him tonight.

Resentment tightened his throat until he could barely swallow. He'd gotten along fine without a mother most of his life. Why did Lyn constantly try to shove his mother down his throat?

He lay for hours, wrestling with questions that had no answers. When he finally slept, his mother's voice haunted his dreams.

When he awoke in the morning, he forced himself to move through his normal routine instead of running down the stairs and grabbing his wife and kissing her senseless until she forgot why she'd been mad at him. As he descended the stairs, a cautious sense of pleasure spread through him as he inhaled the welcome scent of coffee. This might be his favorite part of the day, this moment when Lyn handed him his first cup of coffee and he held her against him for a few moments. And if she thought this morning was going to be different just because they'd had their first fight, she was in for a big surprise.

But she wasn't in the kitchen. His coffee was still in

the pot, freshly dripped thanks to the timer. On the counter lay a note.

Cal—I volunteered to take Mrs. Jenssen to the airport in Rapid. Your lunch is in the fridge. We have to talk this evening. Lyn

His pleasure in the day evaporated. The note was businesslike in its simplicity, not a word of intimacy. It could have been written by an employee.

Guilt struck. Wasn't that essentially what he'd told Lyn she was?

How in hell had things gone so wrong between them? On his wedding night, and every night since, he'd felt like the luckiest man in the world. He needed Lyn to make him complete. Didn't she realize that? Though he hadn't fully realized it until he'd slipped his ring on her finger and heard her soft, husky voice repeating their wedding vows, *he needed her.*

His heart was racing and his chest was tight as he re-read the terse note. Talk? About what? Was she leaving him? Last night's ultimatum had slipped out of his mouth before he could stop it. Even then, he hadn't been able to utter the word ''leave.'' He was too terrified she'd do it.

He stared at the door, unseeing, with dry, burning eyes. His life had finally seemed perfect. He was a rancher again, something he'd wanted almost since the day he left South Dakota as a miserable teenager. He had a ranch that promised to do reasonably well, and he'd found the woman he'd been looking for his entire life to share it with him.

The woman he'd been looking for his entire life. Lyn, with her quiet competence, her graceful presence, her soft, sweet body and the way she became a wildcat in his arms. She loved him, he was sure. It might have started out as gratitude for giving her a home, but he didn't really care as long as she never stopped loving him. He wished she'd told him how she felt, but then why would she? He'd made her think she was no more important to him than a valuable ranch hand.

The room suddenly seemed cold, and he shivered. If she left him he didn't know what he'd do.

My God, he loved her. He'd never intended to let himself open to loving someone, never intended to give someone the power to shatter his life as his mother had shattered his father's. But he hadn't had a choice. She'd sneaked into his heart and blown down all his carefully placed fences and now he didn't think he could live without her.

If she left him it would be one more thing in his life to blame his mother for.

As soon as the thought entered his head, he knew it wasn't fair. Lyn would tell him he was a better man than to have petty thoughts like that, and he guessed she must be rubbing off on him because even *he* couldn't blame his mother for his current predicament. He'd come out of his office to drive her home last night and found the two women so deep in discussion they'd never even heard him halt just outside the kitchen door.

All his life, he'd heard about the woman who hated South Dakota, who couldn't abide its citizens and who cared so little for her own child that she abandoned him as an infant. He'd visited her in Virginia and seen a woman serene in her environment, apparently perfectly happy with her second family and pleased to include him in the charmed circle on a temporary basis. A woman who'd forgotten all about his father, even though Cal knew his father remembered her every time he looked at the son they'd created together.

Lyn had seen something entirely different when she

looked at his mother, and despite his displeasure, she'd risked her own happiness to show him he'd been wrong.

He'd been wrong! His father had been a good man, but clearly he hadn't been entirely fair to Cal's mother in his recall of their shared past. Lyn was right. His mother surely didn't behave as if she thought she was better than someone like Rilla, who was definitely a diamond in the rough. The memory of the devastation in Cora Lee's voice when she'd spoken of leaving him behind pierced his heart, creating for the first time a small opening, like the abscess in the gelding's hoof, through which the poison and bitterness that had infected his system for so many years began to drain.

He closed his eyes. He wanted to share his moment of truth with Lyn, but after the things he'd said last night, he was afraid she'd think he was just mouthing the words so she wouldn't leave.

Tonight, he promised himself. Tonight, he and Lyn were going to have a long talk. A talk that included words like *love* and *forgive,* words like forever. He'd start over with his mother, make up for the years he'd held back. Lyn would be cleared of the charges of murder just as soon as they figured out who had killed her husband, because he knew with every fiber of his being that she couldn't have done it.

He paused, something nagging at the back of his mind. The day of their wedding they'd stopped at the police station. Biddle and Amick, the detectives, had questioned Lyn, and she'd told them about the dreams. The dreams…there was something about the dreams…

And then he knew what it was. And his blood ran cold.

On an impulse, he picked up the phone and called the Pennington County Sheriff's Department. Amick answered the phone in the investigations division.

"Where's your partner?" Cal asked peremptorily after he'd identified himself.

There was a silence. "He's taking some personal leave," Amick answered cautiously. "Why do you want to know?"

"Because I think the son of a bitch killed a man, and he might be after my wife."

There was a sharp intake of breath on the other end. "Tell me," said the detective. "We need to know everything you know. Your wife's life might depend on it."

"It was right under your nose," Cal told him roughly. "The last time we were in, when Lyn mentioned her dreams, she never said anything about where she was hiding. And yet your good buddy Biddle asked her, "How did you get out of the closet and get away?"

"Damn," Amick said. "I can't believe I missed it. We've been investigating him for some high-stakes gambling activity, which I suspect is how Galloway got involved."

Amick's tone was infused with urgency when he spoke again. "Mr. McCall, keep your wife within sight at all times until I personally contact you again."

"I can't." Cal's voice was flat. "She drove my mother to the airport in Rapid this morning."

"We have to assume he might have been watching for a chance to get her alone," Amick said. "Let me make a few calls for manpower and we'll start looking right away."

"I'm doing the same," Cal informed him. "And you'd better hope you find him first."

Amick drew in another sharp breath. "I can't advocate vigilantism, McCall—"

"Then don't. Just get busy."

"McCall." There was a pause. "He drives a dark blue Ford."

Cal exhaled resolutely. "Thanks." And he cut the connection. His heart was pounding; adrenaline rushed through him. The thought of Lyn and his mother in the hands of a cold-blooded killer twisted his gut into knots, and he forced the panic from his mind, coolly concentrating on what he needed to do.

He called Deck, Marty and his cowboys. They spread out over the highways, moving toward Murdo, toward Interior, toward Martin and Midland and over every other halfway decent road, looking for the silver pickup Lyn would be driving. He took off along the route she should have used, taking I-90 straight to Rapid City.

She shouldn't have much of a head start on him, if any, because Silver told him he'd just missed them when he called. So he floored the gas pedal well beyond the legal limit, rocketing down the interstate at nearly ninety. This early in the morning, there wasn't another vehicle in sight.

Gambling. *Damn,* he thought in disgust. Lyn had nearly been killed, was in danger *now* because her ex-husband had been too stupid to control his betting. If the man wasn't already dead...

As he drew closer to Wall, he caught sight of a familiar truck well ahead of him, cresting a rise and disappearing over the other side. He increased his speed even more—

And that's when he saw the dark-colored sedan right behind the truck.

In the distance behind him, the rising wail of a cop's siren shattered the air.

Cal cursed vividly. Who knew what Biddle might do if this became a high-speed chase? He had to get Lyn out of the way of harm.

As he closed the gap between his own truck and the two vehicles ahead, the cop car closed in on him. Lyn appeared to be driving at a sedate sixty-something, well under the speed limit. Probably because of his mother, he thought with a touch of humor. She'd repeatedly expressed horrified amazement at the legal speed limit and the laissez-faire attitude South Dakotans took toward wearing seat belts. He hoped to hell both women were wearing them today.

Biddle's blue sedan was directly behind Lyn, and with a sense of utter fury, Cal could see where bullets had shattered the back window—

What the— Cal ducked and swore as the right side of his windshield shattered. Biddle had shot at him!

With a growl of rage, he floored the truck's gas again, roaring up behind the slower-moving vehicles. He eased off the gas as he closed the gap, praying that Lyn was unharmed, that she was prepared for the action unfolding in her rearview mirror.

She must have been watching, because she suddenly slammed on the brakes. Biddle reacted instinctively, hitting his brakes while Lyn cut the silver truck hard toward the median. Biddle skidded and tried to follow but the blue sedan wasn't as heavy as her truck and he nearly rolled it over. Cal caught a glimpse of the man's frantic face as he tried to turn the wheel and keep hold of a large, steely gray pistol clutched in his right hand. Cal reacted immediately, stomping on his brake pedal, but his wheels locked and he began to skid—

And then his pickup slammed heavily into the side of the sedan, the impact squarely catching the driver's side door.

Metal screeched and tires screamed across the road's surface. Cal felt himself slammed forward and back, arms and legs and head banging painfully against truck parts, glass showering him. The seat belt bit into his hipbones so hard it felt like it was tearing him in half, and both doors on the truck flew open.

And then, just as abruptly, all movement stopped.

He didn't wait to assess his injuries, didn't wait for anything. His fingers tore at the seat belt buckle and he threw himself out of the crazily listing open door, staggering as his feet hit the asphalt. It was only a few strides to where the front of his truck and Biddle's car were entwined in a deadly lovers' embrace of metal. He could see the man, lying unmoving in his seat belt, slumped to the right with his head twisted on his neck at a physically impossible angle.

Abruptly, he stopped. The sight was sickening, even to a man used to doctoring and butchering his own stock. A woman's voice behind him made him spin as he remembered his wife and his mother. Lyn's truck had swerved to a hasty stop in the median, and both women were rushing toward him. Quickly, he moved to intercept them before they could see the dead man.

His heart was still pounding, but the red mist of rage that had driven him was fading beneath the horror and shock of the accident.

As he reached the grass, he opened his arms and folded them both to him, feeling a sense of relief so deep that his knees buckled and he slid down onto the grass with both women still in his arms. For a long moment, the trio knelt there, clutching each other.

"He—he was shooting at us!" Cora Lee stuttered indignantly.

Lyn's face was buried in his throat. "How did you know?" she asked, her lips moving against his skin. He tightened his arm around her, uncaring that the action made his ribs scream with pain; an objective part of him suspected something might be cracked or broken.

"The day we got married," he managed to say, "he asked you about hiding in the closet. But you'd never told any of us where you were hiding. I didn't remember it until this morning," he said, mentally kicking himself.

"He must have been terrified I'd remember everything and blow the whistle on him," she said.

"Cal, you're hurt." His mother's hands tilted his chin up for a gentle inspection. "You need a doctor." She rose to her feet. "Paramedics," she shouted in an authoritative tone at the cop who was by now examining the accident scene. "My son needs medical attention!"

Lyn lifted her head, and they both stared at Cora Lee. She stared back for a moment, and then her brows arched and she smiled sheepishly. "I'm not totally helpless, you know."

They all laughed.

Cal gave her a lopsided grin as he caught at her hand. "I'm all right."

"You most certainly are not." Cora Lee still had her purse over her shoulder and to his amusement, she whipped out a pristine white handkerchief and began to blot at his head. It wasn't until he saw the brilliant red stain on the fabric that he realized blood was dripping into his eyes. He put up a hand and explored the wound.

"It's just a deep scratch, Mama," he said to reassure her.

His mother's hand fell away. She pressed the bloody handkerchief to her chest and as he watched, her eyes slowly filled with tears. "You called me Mama," she whispered.

Lyn's lips moved in a soundless kiss against his throat

as he tugged his mother against him again with his free arm. "I did," he confirmed.

To his annoyance, they took him to Rapid City Regional Hospital in an ambulance. Lyn and Cora Lee followed. Lyn stayed with him while they examined him, and after his head was patched and his ribs were wrapped, he was released with several hundred instructions and an order to rest for a few days.

When they came into the waiting room, Deck and Silver were waiting with his mother. Anxiety gave way to relief—and tears from the women—at his appearance.

After a moment, Deck drew him aside. "There aren't going to be any charges filed," he informed Cal. "The sheriff and some detective came by here while you were being looked over. I'm not sure how they're going to handle the whole thing but they said something about the guy who died driving recklessly."

"Fine with me." He'd considered the possibility that he might stand trial for manslaughter and decided he'd have done exactly the same thing over again, given the situation. Still, he was glad they were going to be understanding.

His truck had been taken to an auto body shop in Rapid, so Lyn drove him home in hers. Deck and Silver took Cora Lee to catch a later flight home, after a final goodbye in which he'd invited her to stay with Lyn and him anytime, and to bring his stepfather along, as well.

He'd refused to take anything for pain, and while the interstate wasn't too bad, the secondary roads and the lane back to the ranch had him fighting not to groan aloud. Despite his disgust with his own weakness, he didn't argue when Lyn ordered him to bed for the rest of the day.

''Where will you be?'' He caught her hand when she made a move to rise from the edge of the bed where she'd been sitting.

She shrugged. ''I have work to do. The stock in the barn needs to be checked and the gelding's foot should be soaked again. I thawed a chicken this morning for dinner, but if I don't get it started roasting, it'll be midnight before we eat. I'll bring you a tray tonight so you don't have to come down.''

''Are you all right?'' he asked quietly. She hadn't said a word the whole way home about the man who'd pursued her.

''Yes.'' She met his eyes. ''I didn't realize he was behind us until we were almost at Wall. And by then...by then, you were there.''

''He shot at you.'' It was almost a snarl.

She nodded and her fingers tightened in his. ''I couldn't believe it. And the funny thing was, I wasn't concerned for myself but I was outraged at the thought that he might hurt your mother. I wanted to kill him!'' Then she realized what she'd said, and her face grew sober. ''I'd be lying if I said I was sorry he's dead. But I'm sad for him, and for Wayne. They were little kids once, with big dreams just like every other child. Isn't it weird how life turns out?''

''It is.'' He caressed the fine-grained skin beneath his fingers. ''If it hadn't been for them, I might never have met you.''

''That's true.'' Lyn tugged her hand free of his, her eyes looking anywhere but at him. ''Well, I really have to get to work, and you should rest for a while.''

And before he could stop her, she was gone.

She didn't sleep with him again that night, or the next one. He was so stiff and sore he knew he couldn't pursue her like he wanted to, so he waited, frustrated and increasingly annoyed, as she avoided any topics other than general ranch-related things.

On the third day, he got up at his usual time. He was moving a little slower than normal, due to all the bruises he'd acquired, but a long, hot shower helped loosen his muscles and soothe the aches, and he emerged feeling more like himself than he had since he realized a madman might be chasing his wife.

As he entered the kitchen, Lyn walked toward him with a steaming mug of coffee. "Good morning." Her smile was warm. "I heard you moving around up there."

"We have to talk." Her smile faded as he set the coffee untouched on the counter and took her hand, towing her after him into the living room. He eased himself down on the couch but when she would have seated herself beside him, he tugged her into his lap.

She started to squirm and protest.

"Stay still or you'll hurt my ribs," he said, shamelessly using his injuries.

She froze, then moved herself carefully into a rigidly upright position so that she wasn't leaning against him.

He promptly pulled her off balance so that she slid sideways against him, her head in the crook of his arm.

She looked up at him with wide eyes. "What are you doing? You need—"

"I *need* my wife." He stressed the verb. "You've been doing your best to keep a distance between us, and I don't just mean a physical one." He lifted his free hand and stroked a finger down the soft curve of her cheek. "What's wrong?"

She closed her eyes. "Nothing. You said you liked the way things between us were comfortable. I've been trying to keep them that way."

"Lyn." It was a warning growl. "Open your eyes."

She ignored him until he put his hand at the top button of her shirt and started opening the fastenings one by one. "Cal! Wait. You can't—"

"Yes, I can," he said, dragging her hand to his lap. She'd always responded to him this way, always been warm and sweet and wild and *loving*. He pulled at her clothes, stopping to fondle her breasts and thumb her nipples into tight little peaks, and she stopped arguing and started helping him.

When she was naked he tore off his own shirt and unfastened his pants and shoved them down. Already aching for her, he took her hips and guided her astride him, closing his eyes and groaning in ecstasy when she took him into her body, easing her down until he was fully sheathed.

She was smiling, a smug feminine expression with her green eyes half-closed in pleasure. He took her hair from its elastic, pulling it over her milky white shoulders and plunging his hands deep into the heavy mass, framing her face between his palms.

"I love you," he said.

Her eyes opened wide, and her lips parted. He flexed his hips beneath her, driving himself more deeply into her.

"I love you," he said again. Then the days of being without her overwhelmed him and he took her by the hips, moving her up and down until she took over the rhythm, sliding herself over him as he explored the rusty thatch of curls between her legs, touching her in the ways he'd learned made her melt in his arms. He felt his body gathering into a taut, shaking knot of need, shivers chasing down his back to center in the pleasured flesh buried snugly within her.

She rode him harder, interpreting his clenched jaw and bunched muscles correctly. "I love you, too," she gasped. Then her body took over, waves of final pleasure breaking over her head, and as he felt her flesh caressing him, he let himself go, pouring everything he was into her, holding her tightly to him with her face buried in his throat as his body arched and bucked beneath her.

There was a long silence in the room afterward. He didn't feel especially inclined to move, though he slowly stroked his hand up and down the satiny length of her spine.

"I don't deserve you," he said softly.

She sat up and her eyes snapped open. "Of course you do," she said in a gentle tone, her husky voice full of emotion.

"No." He put a finger to her lips when she would have spoken further. "Until today, I've never even told you that I love you, that I can't imagine my life without you by my side, and still you gave me everything."

Her pupils expanded so that her exquisite eyes were nearly black. But she didn't say a word. Then tears welled. "I've loved you almost since the day you brought me home," she said.

"I like the way you say that," he informed her. "Home is what this place has become since you arrived." A stab of regret pierced him. "I'm sorry if I made you think all I wanted was a housekeeper who would warm my bed."

"It's all right." She stroked his jaw. "I don't mind making you comfortable."

"That's good." He leaned forward to kiss her on the tip of her nose. "I think I need to spend the day in bed getting comfortable." Lifting her from his lap, he yanked up his jeans, took her hand and started for the stairs, leaving the rest of their clothing strewn over the floor.

Several hours later, he pulled her beneath him yet again. "You know something? I forgot all about birth control today."

Lyn's eyes softened. "Funny you should bring that up. I've been going to mention that very thing to you. I'm not sure we need it anymore."

Cal stilled, looking down at the woman who'd become his world. "Are you—do you think…" He took a deep breath, blew it out. "Tell me."

She smiled at him. "Remember the laundry room?"

He grinned. "Not a memory I'm ever likely to forget. I still can't walk through there without getting—"

She put a hand over his mouth, giggling, brushing her hips against his. "I get the idea." Then she lifted her arms, clasping them around his neck. "I'm not sure," she said. "It's been just over a month now, but I'm usually very regular."

"A baby." He kissed her forehead tenderly. "I thought I wanted to wait, but the thought of seeing you with our child in your arms—" He stopped, overwhelmed. Then he raised his head again. "My God, I love you."

And as she lifted her body to his, he thanked every twist of fate that had sent her into his home and his arms forever.

* * * * *

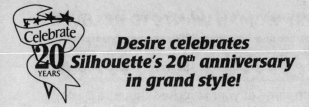
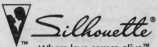 

You're not going to believe this offer!

In October and November 2000, buy any two Harlequin or Silhouette books and save $10.00 off future purchases, or buy any three and save $20.00 off future purchases!

Just fill out this form and attach 2 proofs of purchase (cash register receipts) from October and November 2000 books and Harlequin will send you a coupon booklet worth a total savings of $10.00 off future purchases of Harlequin and Silhouette books in 2001. Send us 3 proofs of purchase and we will send you a coupon booklet worth a total savings of $20.00 off future purchases.

Saving money has never been this easy.

I accept your offer! Please send me a coupon booklet:

Name: _____

Address: _____ City: _____

State/Prov.: _____ Zip/Postal Code: _____

Optional Survey!

In a typical month, how many Harlequin or Silhouette books would you buy <u>new</u> at retail stores?

- ☐ Less than 1   ☐ 1   ☐ 2   ☐ 3 to 4   ☐ 5+

Which of the following statements best describes how you <u>buy</u> Harlequin or Silhouette books? Choose one answer only that <u>best</u> describes you.

- ☐ I am a regular buyer and reader
- ☐ I am a regular reader but buy only occasionally
- ☐ I only buy and read for specific times of the year, e.g. vacations
- ☐ I subscribe through Reader Service but also buy at retail stores
- ☐ I mainly borrow and buy only occasionally
- ☐ I am an occasional buyer and reader

Which of the following statements best describes how you <u>choose</u> the Harlequin and Silhouette series books you buy <u>new</u> at retail stores? By "series," we mean books within a particular line, such as *Harlequin PRESENTS* or *Silhouette SPECIAL EDITION*. Choose one answer only that <u>best</u> describes you.

- ☐ I only buy books from my favorite series
- ☐ I generally buy books from my favorite series but also buy books from other series on occasion
- ☐ I buy some books from my favorite series but also buy from many other series regularly
- ☐ I buy all types of books depending on my mood and what I find interesting and have no favorite series

---

Please send this form, along with your cash register receipts as proofs of purchase, to:
In the U.S.: Harlequin Books, P.O. Box 9057, Buffalo, NY 14269
In Canada: Harlequin Books, P.O. Box 622, Fort Erie, Ontario L2A 5X3
(Allow 4-6 weeks for delivery) Offer expires December 31, 2000.

PHQ4002

where love comes alive—online...

eHARLEQUIN.com

shop eHarlequin

- ♥ Find all the new Silhouette releases at everyday great discounts.
- ♥ Try before you buy! Read an excerpt from the latest Silhouette novels.
- ♥ Write an online review and share your thoughts with others.

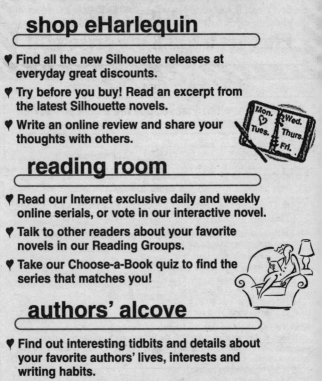

reading room

- ♥ Read our Internet exclusive daily and weekly online serials, or vote in our interactive novel.
- ♥ Talk to other readers about your favorite novels in our Reading Groups.
- ♥ Take our Choose-a-Book quiz to find the series that matches you!

authors' alcove

- ♥ Find out interesting tidbits and details about your favorite authors' lives, interests and writing habits.
- ♥ Ever dreamed of being an author? Enter our Writing Round Robin. The Winning Chapter will be published online! Or review our writing guidelines for submitting your novel.

If you enjoyed what you just read,
then we've got an offer you can't resist!

Take 2 bestselling
love stories FREE!

Plus get a FREE surprise gift!

Clip this page and mail it to Silhouette Reader Service™

IN U.S.A.	IN CANADA
3010 Walden Ave.	P.O. Box 609
P.O. Box 1867	Fort Erie, Ontario
Buffalo, N.Y. 14240-1867	L2A 5X3

YES! Please send me 2 free Silhouette Desire® novels and my free surprise gift. Then send me 6 brand-new novels every month, which I will receive months before they're available in stores. In the U.S.A., bill me at the bargain price of $3.34 plus 25¢ delivery per book and applicable sales tax, if any*. In Canada, bill me at the bargain price of $3.74 plus 25¢ delivery per book and applicable taxes**. That's the complete price and a savings of at least 10% off the cover prices—what a great deal! I understand that accepting the 2 free books and gift places me under no obligation ever to buy any books. I can always return a shipment and cancel at any time. Even if I never buy another book from Silhouette, the 2 free books and gift are mine to keep forever. So why not take us up on our invitation. You'll be glad you did!

225 SEN C222
326 SEN C223

Name	(PLEASE PRINT)	
Address	Apt.#	
City	State/Prov.	Zip/Postal Code

* Terms and prices subject to change without notice. Sales tax applicable in N.Y.
** Canadian residents will be charged applicable provincial taxes and GST.
All orders subject to approval. Offer limited to one per household.
® are registered trademarks of Harlequin Enterprises Limited.

DES00 ©1998 Harlequin Enterprises Limited

Silhouette® Desire®

COMING NEXT MONTH

#1327 MARRIAGE PREY—Annette Broadrick
Until she found herself stranded on an isolated island with irresistibly handsome police detective Steve Antonelli, red-hot passion had just been one of overprotected Robin McAlister's fantasies. Could her sizzling romance with an experienced man like Steve develop into a lasting love?

#1328 HER PERFECT MAN—Mary Lynn Baxter
Man of the Month
Strong-willed minister Bryce Burnette and flamboyant Katherine Mays couldn't have been more different. Only the fierce desire and tender love this red-haired beauty was stirring up inside Bryce would be able to dissolve the barriers that separated them.

#1329 A COWBOY'S GIFT—Anne McAllister
Code of the West
Rodeo cowboy Gus Holt had to do a whole lot more than turn on his legendary charm if he wanted to win back the heart of schoolteacher Mary McLean. He'd have to prove—in a very special way—that this time he was offering her a lifetime of love.

#1330 HUSBAND—OR ENEMY?—Caroline Cross
Fortune's Children: The Grooms
Angelica Dodd was powerfully drawn to—and pregnant by—charismatic bad boy Riley Fortune. But trusting him was another matter. Could Riley open his hardened heart and show her that they shared more than a marriage of convenience?

#1331 THE VIRGIN AND THE VENGEFUL GROOM—Dixie Browning
The Passionate Powers/Body & Soul
Even his tough training as a navy SEAL hadn't given Curt Powers the wherewithal to resist a virginal beauty like Lily O'Malley. He longed to take Lily—to make her his woman. But much to this confirmed bachelor's surprise, he also wanted to make her his *wife*.

#1332 NIGHT WIND'S WOMAN—Sheri WhiteFeather
The moment pregnant Kelly Baxter showed up at his door, Shane Night Wind knew his life was forever changed. How could he walk away from this woman in need? How could he protect his heart when Kelly and her baby could be his only salvation?

CMN1000